HIDDEN DREAMS

BARBARA ELAINE RATNER ROSEN

ACKNOWLEDGMENTS

Foremost I must express my gratitude to my first creative writing teacher Eva Bromberg, who encouraged me to remain in the "group" and taught me the basics of writing.

Pearl Sauerhaft, Betty Vallone, Oscar White, Jim Lilly, James Laverty, Bernadette Carson and Libby Klein became my writing "buddies" and critique mavens. Their remarks and positive attitude provided me with the impetus to forge ahead in the right direction.

Mention has to be made to the late Bernadette Carson, who cajoled and helped me expand my little story into this novel.

Thank you my dear friend Libby for your interest and positive outlook in this endeavor.

Thanks Catherine McBurn, you certainly corrected my English.

To my expert finisher, Rich Gold. Thank you!

-1-

Sam finished his dinner and brought his coffee into the garden. He sat on a favorite old green striped beach chair, his foot resting on the worn nylon material. From this position, he had a complete view of the flora. The plantings were arranged so that something would always be in bloom. This summer evening, the red and yellow roses and purple pansies circled a bed of white daises with lemon- yellow centers. Floating water lilies protected the fish in a small pond. Impatiens in alternating shades of purple, violet, and red surrounded the pond. Red, orange, and white geraniums filled large wooden pots on each corner of the patio. The panoply of color in the garden gave Sam a peaceful satisfied feeling. "I love this garden, especially during this time of day," Sam said to no one in particular.

The sun began its decline; the sky splattered with red as if on fire.
"Jeanne, come enjoy the sunset!" Sam called.

"What a sight," she said, making herself comfortable in the matching chair while reaching for his hand.

They sat quietly side by side. He looked adoringly at her. The couple seemed well suited to each other. The empty cup slipped onto Sam's stomach as he started to doze. Halfway between sleep and reality he thought about the first time he had seen Jeanne.

Sam had been playing softball in Central Park on a spring Sunday morning in 1962. As he swayed, swinging his bat in practice, his eyes locked with the pretty blonde girl sitting in the stands. He smiled and turned back to business. Trying hard to impress her, he struck out, hanging his head in embarrassment, though the next time at bat, he hit the winning run. As Sam rounded home, he glanced to make sure she saw him. She did. After the game, Sam went to the stands and introduced himself.

"Sam I am!" he laughed.

"Hi, I'm Jeanne," she responded with a shy smile.

"How about getting some coffee?" Sam asked.

"Sure," she beamed.

He remembered how they had talked for hours and at the end of the evening knew it was love at first sight. Less than one year later, they married, and it's been forty years since that special day.

Jeanne took the empty cup as she watched Sam snore away. "How many nights have I listened to the sounds he makes while he sleeps? A lifetime together," she muttered sarcastically. "But he's a fine man. We've had a good life. But there must be more to it." Jeanne breathed a long sigh as she looked at her garden. They had planted this rainbow of colors together as they had done so many other things over the years, she mused. With her eyes closed, she wondered where the years had gone. Where was the spark? The fire seemed to have smoldered. We've become complacent with each other; never go dancing, no more romantic interludes; no more touchy feely, she mused.

*

The ringing of the telephone broke her reverie. Jeanne rose abruptly and ran to answer it.

"Hello," she said, breathlessly, lifting the receiver.

"Hi Hon," the male voice said. "Can you talk?"

"He's sleeping," Jeanne whispered.

"I'm here; I miss you and want you. How about tomorrow?" he asked in a lusty voice.

"Twelve o'clock at our usual place?" Jeanne asked. "Sam will be playing in his regular golf game."

"I can hardly wait to hold you," he replied. "I'll be counting the hours till we are together."

"Me too," Jeanne murmured happily.

She hung up the phone, returned to her chair with the smile of a Cheshire cat, and closed her eyes thinking of tomorrow.

-2-

Jeanne opened the door to Suite 711 of the Hilton Hotel. She drove from her home to the next town, as Marty suggested, so that she would not be recognized. Marty waited with open arms. He enveloped her and showered her with kisses. The lights were dim. The wine cooled in the caddie. Her favorite piano- etude filled the room. The scene was set.

She looked around and felt warm in the honey beige monochromatic room. The couch and soft armchairs welcomed her. Straight ahead the bedroom beckoned them. As their eyes met, they threw their clothes askew on the plush flowered rug and came together on the king size bed with soft fluffy pillows to comfort them. Marty caressed Jeanne tenderly whispering words of love in her ear. He professed his feelings for her as they consummated their passion.

Relaxed in the comfortable bed, with Jeanne's head resting on his chest, Marty gave her a hug and said, "Love, we're made for each other. We must always be together as we are now. Our time is special."

"Do you mean you're ready to leave your wife?" she whispered, raising her head to look into his eyes.

"Well nooooo," he stammered, looking away. "I meant we should remain as we are. I'll call you every time I'm in town."

The silence was deafening. He took a deep breath and continued, "Anyway you don't want to leave Sam either. Why spoil a good thing? We have the best of both worlds; our families and each other."

Knowing that he would never leave his wife, and with a stab of conscience, Jeanne said sadly, "What we have now is deceit. It's dishonest."

"No, no honey, we're not hurting anyone. We actually make our marriages better with our dalliance. Since Betty and Sam are boring and ordinary, this spices the juices up and makes life bearable. I would leave Betty, but she needs me. I can't hurt her. The children couldn't adjust.

'And plain old Sam, with his golf games, his garden and books, has little time for you. Where does he ever take you? You want this diversion. But he still needs you and probably couldn't survive without you. Let's not change anything. This way we're all happy. Me especially," he chuckled.

Marty took Jeanne's silence as reassuring and thought *I'm glad we cleared that up*. "Hon let's not quarrel. We still have time. Let's saunter back to bed. It's so inviting."

"Marty, how about lunch?"

"Fine after we make love, we'll order room service."

"I mean, let's go out for lunch."

"Are you nuts? You forget that I could be recognized. What would I tell Betty? Anyway, room service here is great."

Jeanne's mood changed from loving to angry. "What about me? Don't I count for anything? Am I just a trinket? It's been six months since we're together and what have I got to show for it? A few afternoons of sexual pleasure," she cried, elaborating each word. Tears flowed down her face in black streaks of mascara. She ran into the bathroom, slammed the door, looked at her reflection in the mirror, and saw herself for what she had become. A cheat! A liar!

"Jeanne, come out. Let's talk. I love you," Marty said in a low soft voice.

Jeanne pondered! "I'm starting to see this affair for what it really is. Lust not love!" She washed her face, took a deep breath, opened the door and with a smile on her face, calmly walked into the bedroom. He followed, untying his robe while reaching for her, thinking, whew her tantrum is over.

Jeanne stopped. She looked right at him, her blue eyes cold and unemotional. She gathered her clothes and dressed. Marty's face dropped, with his mouth hanging.

"What're you doing?" he said in a panic. "Where are you going? What's so important that it infringes on our time together?" His voice raised an octave. His cold eyes and the tightness of his jaw revealed the anger he felt.

She returned to the living room and picked up her shoes and jacket. "It took me a long time, but I finally realize my role in this arrangement," Jeanne lamented. "Keeping you happy? Me! Me is all I hear. This affair is as boring as you say my life is. We never go outside. No dinners out. No theater. No dancing. Only the bed and this room! At least Sam is not afraid to be seen with me. There's something to be said for sharing a lifetime together. There is no rainbow here.

'It began as fun, but the fun has become a drudge. I've been sensing this for some time now. I was looking for something wonderful and now realize I've had it all along. I will make my life interesting on my terms- not yours. Life is good and I'm lucky to have it with a man who loves me and wants the best for me and not just for himself. I've been foolish. It took me a long time to see this, and I am grateful to you for pointing it out to me. If you weren't so selfish, I would never have learned this lesson. Thanks for that."

Jeanne kissed him lightly on the lips, patted his cheek, picked up her Gucci, and walked out of the hotel room. A bewildered Marty, with a shocked look on his face, stood by the open door.

-3-

"Sam, I'm home!" Jeanne called as she opened the door to their garden. Sam sat in his usual chair, this overweight, balding man, with his half reading glasses hanging on his nose, reading Hemingway's *A Farewell To Arms*. An avid reader he had a tendency to reread his favorite books. Jeanne glanced at the title as she bent to kiss him on his forehead. She thought, with a smile, *how can he read the same book again? He must have read it ten times. That's Sam. A few days ago I would have shown my irritation, but today the sameness comforts me.*

"Let's go for a late lunch," Jeanne suggested. "I'm starving."

"Sure," Sam surprisingly said. "We usually eat home, so it'll be nice. I'll change and we'll go to the beach and eat on the pier."

*

As they sipped their Bloody Marys waiting for the food, Sam asked? "Did you have a nice morning dear?"

"It was O.K.," Jeanne answered as she looked out of the window.

"I didn't see any packages. Did you buy anything?"

"No, no nothing hit my eye"

"How about Joan? What did she get?"

"Uh, she bought a pants outfit and a bag to match," she lied nervously as she played with the celery stick in her drink.

The food arrived before this uncomfortable conversation could continue. There was an awkward silence as they ate. Jeanne toyed with her sea bass while Sam concentrated on his snapper. Over cappuccino, Sam started his banter again.

"Was there traffic on the way to the mall? I heard there was an accident on the highway."

"Yes. A l-i-t-t-l-e. Although it wasn't too bad," Jeanne stammered skeptically, not knowing the real answer.

"Did you meet any friends?"

Jeanne squirmed in the chair. *Sam is not usually so inquisitive. Most of the time he hardly notices I'm gone.* She skillfully changed the subject, talking about a new Oprah book she was reading, *"The House of Sand and Fog."*

*

They arrived home a few hours later to a ringing telephone. Jeanne answered it only to hear Marty's voice.

"I need you," he wailed.

"What do you want?" she responded quietly.

"I need you," he cried again, only much louder. "Come back to me."

"Honey, who is it?" Sam yelled. "... for me?"

"Don't call here again," she whispered emphatically, "Or I'll call Betty."

"No Sam, it was an insurance agent. I told him we weren't interested."

The phone rang again. She rushed to answer it. No one spoke on the other end, only breathing.

"Wrong number," she said weakly.

The shrill continuous ringing caused Jeanne's heart to flutter. Each time she picked it up, with no response from the other end. She said loudly, "Stop calling or I will call the police," knowing full well that she wouldn't. She knew who it was and didn't know how to handle it without involving Sam. Jeanne silently prayed for Marty to stop calling.

Sam said, "Why don't we call the police to report these crank calls?"

"Let's ignore them," she feebly acknowledged.

Sam ran to pick the receiver up on the next ring. Jeanne stopped breathing.

Sam yelled, "Hello."

"Sam, what's wrong? It's only me, Joan."

"Sorry. We've been getting crank calls."

Jeanne gave a sigh of relief even though she didn't know who was on the other end.

"How are you Joan? You just left Jeanne. What do you two have so much to say to each other?"

"Just saw her? You're getting forgetful. That was two days ago."

"Sorry, I must be mistaken," he said, turning pale.

He handed the phone to Jeanne without saying a word and walked out to the garden. He took a deep breath, inhaled the fragrance of his flowers, and tried to calm himself, as he picked up his book.

A few minutes later Jeanne sheepishly came out. Sam appeared to be reading. "Don't say anything," he said without lifting his head. "Lies, lies all around us," he cried through clenched teeth. "Do you really think I don't know about you and that guy? Shopping two or three times a week is not your style. You always say I hate shopping. Stores are too crowded. Things are too expensive. BUT right after Christmas, when there was nothing left to buy, you started to shop. For what? No packages. Did you think I wouldn't notice? I might not talk much, but I do notice. Last week I stooped so low as to hire an investigator to have you followed."

"Sam, I-"

"I patiently waited for you to talk to me about it," he interrupted gruffly. "I thought our marriage was honest enough for you to confide in me that you weren't happy."

In defeat, his eyes reflected his sadness, looking blankly at his flowers, blinking back the tears.

Jeanne hesitantly came toward him. "What can I say? I'm sorry. I made a big mistake. Please -"

Before she could finish, he lashed out. "Not now. I need time. Go away."

She didn't know what to do and stood there feeling numb. *What will happen*, she thought? *Does he mean it? Should I go away?* Scared and trembling, glued to the ground, eyes looking up at the sky. She looked at Sam who also seemed to be watching the sun drop behind the horizon. Silence permeated. "What will happen to us?" she mumbled, hardly aware she had spoken.

"Sam," she whispered.

The phone rang. With trepidation, Jeanne answered it.

"Hi Mom," Sara, the thirty-something married daughter, said in a cheery voice. "What's up?"

"Nothing much, sweetheart! All is well," she stammered wearily, having a hard time holding the receiver.

They spoke of nothing in particular and after a few strained minutes, Jeanne hung up and retreated to the den. Alone in the solitude of the walnut paneled room, she stared blankly at the TV. At ten o'clock she heard Sam go up to the bedroom. He had sat in the garden all these hours, she thought. How awful for him. She went upstairs and got ready for bed. Both carefully avoided each other. Jeanne completed her nightly ritual and got into bed. They barely muttered "goodnight," turning their backs to each other.

-4-

The next few days were silent between them. The weather turned cold and damp, with the threat of rain matching the dismal attitudes in the house. One evening during dinner, Jeanne said "Enough, Sam. This behavior *cannot* go on."

Sam sighed and put down the knife and fork he was using to play with his food. "What do you want me to do?" he asked. "I can't look at you without visualizing you with him. I can't. I thought we had a good marriage. I'm at a loss for words. What now?" he said angrily.

Jeanne sobbed, stood up and moved towards him. "I'm so sorry. Can't we get past this? I really love you and wouldn't ever jeopardize that love again." She stopped short as Sam spoke.

"I need some time," Sam said in a monotone voice coated with ice. "I'm going to the lake house for the weekend. I need to be alone to sort things out."

Jeanne spent a lonely weekend roaming from room to room, trying not to call Sam. She barely ate, or even allowed herself the pleasure of a hot bubble bath. She was consumed with guilt and a fear of the future. The quiet was unnerving and she talked to herself. "If I have to give up my marriage what will I do? How will I live without Sam? I always wanted more from life, but now...?" Rambling, she asked, "No more phone calls? Marty must be scared I'll call Betty. I should call her. He deserves that," her voice raised in anger. Exhausted she finally sat down at the kitchen table and attempted to read the Sunday Times.

*

In the meantime, three hours away Sam himself paced back and forth in the summer cottage they both loved so much. *How can I face her after making such a scene he thought? I acted so holier-than-thou. How can I blame her? Am I not as guilty? Didn't I do the same thing some twenty years ago when I traveled selling my fabrics?* He sat down in the rocking chair on the porch facing the lake, his face in his hands, remembering days gone by. Was it different? Was there really a double standard?

Eyes closed, rocking slowly, he reminisced. *Two lonely souls, Katherine and me having drinks in the lounge of the Metropolitan Hotel. How lovely and regal she looked, in her three-piece black suit. The immediate attraction between us! The elevator ride to her room; and our coming together. What an exciting time, an illicit affair. For almost a year Katherine and I planned our trips simultaneously, winding up in the same city at least once a month. How lucky our wares complimented each other; my fabrics and her designs.*

It never spoiled my time together with Jeanne. I loved her so much. I wonder what the outcome would have been had Katherine not been promoted and remained in Chicago? I guess I was lucky things worked out so well.

Then that other time, a few years later, that buyer I met at a trade show. A couple of romps in the sack-- nothing special -- one, two, three -- a few months -- over.

Looking out at the loons cavorting on the lake he said aloud, as if talking to them, "What should I do? How could I make up with her? Dare I tell her about me?" Sam was in a turmoil trying to save his marriage and yet having to deal with a hurt ego. What did I do wrong that she needed this other guy? No answers. No solution. He remained in a quandary.

-5-

On Sunday night Jeanne was watching "60 Minutes", without really seeing it, when the doorbell rang. She opened the door hoping to see Sam, thinking he had forgotten his keys, only to find herself face to face with Betty Silva, Marty's wife.

"I'm Betty," she said haughtily, hands on hips.

Jeanne remained silent shaking like a leaf, eyes wide, with a shocked expression on her face.

"I just want to see what you look like," Betty said.

"How did you, uh...find me?"

"I've had lots of practice. Do you think you're the first? Sorry Hon, you have to stand in line. The son-of-a-bitch thinks he's a stud."

"Why do you stay with him?" Jeanne whimpered, fighting the tears welling in her eyes.

"I love the bastard, even though I would like to kill him," she chuckled in a crazy cackle. "I used to be devastated, but now I look the other way. He always comes back to me. I'm scared to be alone. This way is better."

"I'm so sorry," Jeanne cried. "I seem to be saying that a lot lately. But I really mean it. I'm so ashamed. As a woman I should know better."

Betty screamed in a shrill voice, "He will come back to me you know, so I advise you to give him up. By the way, I will fight for him," she said with a wild look in her eyes. "Although heaven knows why! Don't think you can have him. I'll finish you both if I have to," she continued, rambling. "You have a daughter. What will she think of Mommy sleeping around?"

"No, no it's done," Jeanne said apologetically. "I promise."

Betty whirled around, walked back to her car, yelling "Remember I will fight for him!" She turned back towards Jeanne shaking her fist in a threatening motion. "Remember!"

Jeanne recoiled, as if slapped, and stood in the door repeating, "I'm sorry. I'm so sorry," as the car pulled away with the tires screeching.

*

Tuesday morning Sam came home to an empty house. "Jeanne … Jeanne..," he called as he looked into every room. "Where could she have gone?" he said as the phone rang. Answering it a high pitched female voice spat out, "Where is she? He didn't come, home last night. Did she...? I'll kill them."

"Whoa, slow down," Sam said. "Who is this?" knowing full well who it was.

"I don't have to tell you," Betty said, her voice breaking. She started to cry. "Where is he?"

"Calm down," Sam said in a quiet voice buying time while trying to calm down himself. He started to sweat. "I don't know where anyone is."

"Liar," she screamed slamming the telephone down.

Visibly shaken, Sam plopped into a chair. Did Jeanne really go with him again? How will I handle this? Where could they be? He sat staring.

After a while, he got up, holding on to the chair like an old man who had lost his strength. He looked up the numbers of her friends, in the phone book on the counter, calling each one to ask if she was with them. Defeated, he poured himself a shot glass of scotch, downing it in one gulp. Followed by two more in quick succession, feeling no pain, he collapsed on the couch falling into a stupor- like sleep.

The sun shining through the window woke him. "Jeanne," he called out. He shook himself awake. The silence brought him back to reality, remembering that she wasn't home. With a mouth that tasted like the bottom of a bird cage, he went into the kitchen to get a glass of orange juice. The sudden sound of the garage door opening and the din of the car motor caused him to drop the glass in the sink, smashing it into a thousand pieces.

Jeanne walked into the kitchen looking weary.

Spinning around to face her he cried out, "Where were you? You couldn't stay away from him, could you? You said it was over!" he yelled, pointing his finger at her. "It didn't take you long to go back. What do you need him for?" Sam's voice, laced with anger, broke.

"What are you talking about?" Jeanne asked bewildered. "Go with who? I was at Sara's. I couldn't stay here alone anymore, and I didn't know when you would come home, if ever."

"But, Betty said......"

"Betty, Betty said what?" she interrupted in a raised voice. "Betty was here?"

"She called and said you were with him."

"You have so little faith in me. I thought you knew me better. When I say it's over, I mean it," she said disgustedly.

"Jeanne," he sobbed. "I'm crazy with jealousy. I can't think straight. I can't eat. I can't sleep. I'm nuts," he said walking towards her. "I can't put it out of my mind, you and another man. What should I do?"

Wearily she answered in a voice barely audible, "Twenty years-- both times -- I forgot. In time you will too."

"You knew?" he whispered. The color drained out of his face, his eyes filled with tears. "How? You never let on. All these years…"

"A wife knows. There were tell tale signs; a woman's smell, lipstick stains, hotel receipts. I waited and hoped you would sow your oats and come back to Sara and me. I loved you then and I love you now. I was so hurt I could never talk about it. Life is funny, she said, shaking her head. "Knowing such hurt, how could I put you through that pain?" She walked towards him with her arms open wide and embraced him. He hugged her, breathed in her familiar spicy fragrance, and caressed her face and hair. Eyes locked they kissed long and deep.

-6-

After Sam's confession of his long ago extra- marital affair, Jeanne tried but a wall grew between them. They ate their dinners in silence and slept in separate bedrooms. She felt his attitude regarding her liaison hypocritical since his past wasn't so clean. The only way she could handle her own guilt was to put herself on the defensive.

Sam was distraught about their cold war. They barely spoke and went their separate ways. Jeanne volunteered long hours at the hospital; Sam tended his garden.

During dinner one evening, Sam attempted a truce. "Jeanne, what's going to be with us? I love you. We've had our problems before. We've also had a lifetime behind us. Memories together! Doesn't that count for anything?"

She put her silverware down softly, and looked into his eyes. "Sam, I do miss you," she said in a voice husky with emotion. Her eyes filled with tears.

Without even waiting for an answer, Sam said gently, "I've made reservations for a week in Aruba. Maybe we can recapture what we had."

Jeanne smiled and got up to go to him, glad that her imposed silence would finally end. "Let's go. I have a good feeling about this," she said, hugging him.

*

Jeanne and Sam spent a week on the island of Aruba, trying to rekindle their relationship. They were together, just the two of them. They had breakfast in the privacy of their terrace, drank strong hot coffee and ate delicious fresh baked muffins spread with creamy butter. The surrounding gardens released a sweet fragrance, reminding them of home. The bright colors of the flowers were breathtaking.

Being good swimmers, they swam laps across the Olympic size pool after breakfast. Then they spent the afternoons on the beach lolling in the sun on the white sand and sipped the drink of the islands refreshing rum swizzles. Jeanne read under an umbrella, while in the sun Sam relaxed on a lounge and eventually dozed.

Dinners were in the hotel restaurant. They indulged in Dom Perignon champagne, toasting each other and dancing to the slow music on the patio in the moonlight. The romantic ambiance helped them find their love again. They discovered it had never left; it just went astray.

They couldn't wait to get back in their room where they made love as if they were young. They slept entwined in each others' arms in the middle of the king size bed.

One morning, Jeanne suggested going sailing.

"Good idea," Sam responded.

They rented a sailboat and Sam took the wheel.

"Let's not go out too far," Jeanne suggested. "You haven't sailed for years."

"It's like riding a bike. You never forget," Sam smiled with a confident voice.

They sailed slowly in calm waters under a bright blue sunny sky when Jeanne pointed to the right. "Let's stop on that island. We can eat our lunch there."

Sam steered the boat close to land until the water was too shallow. "We have to swim," he said shutting off the motor. They had to tread water for a short distance. Sam held the basket with one hand above his head, until he was able to stand and walked onto the beach.

They sat on the sand and gazed out at the horizon as they ate their lunch, turkey sandwiches on baguettes, and sipped cold beers. The hot sun made them tired. They dozed, wrapped in each other's arms.

Jeanne suddenly woke feeling chilled. She noticed how dark the sky had become. She shook Sam awake. "Hurry, the weather has changed. A storm is coming."

The palm trees swayed in the wind. The churning waves made the swim to the boat difficult. When they reached the boat, the downpour was hard and the drops pelted their skin. Sam tried to start the motor. His wet hands kept slipping, and he soon flooded the engine. He and Jeanne tried to put the sail down, but the boat swayed so hard that it was impossible. The material billowed from the wind, causing the boat to slip on its end. The sail tore.

They were frightened, not knowing what to do. There was no radio on board, and their cell phones were water soaked. In their excitement they forgot to look for life jackets. After several more attempts the motor turned over, and they started to move. Sam tried to keep the boat steady, but a huge wave flipped it over and they sunk under water. Sam surfaced and yelled, "Jeanne!" over and over with no response. The high waves kept knocking him down, causing him to sink under the water. He found it more difficult to keep himself afloat and began ingesting the raging water.

Desperately fighting the water, he made his way towards the boat. It was lying on its side. He was losing the battle as he grew more exhausted, and he found it harder to catch his breath. Each time he dropped beneath the water it took him longer to emerge. The water clouded his eyes. He could hardly see—panic set in. Barely able to lift his arms he thought, *this is it. I'm done.* An inner strength, that Sam didn't realize he had, kept him from yielding.

The storm suddenly, abated as quickly as it began. The water calmed, and he climbed aboard the rim of the capsized boat. He held on for dear life. Catching his breath, Sam scoured the horizon on all sides looking for Jeanne. Still short of breath, he drew upon all his strength and yelled in a hoarse voice, "Jeanne, Jeanne, Jeanne!" Silence! The only sound he heard was his heart beating against his chest, as if it would jump out of his body. Crying, he instinctively tried to think how to save himself. Shivering and shaking, he held onto the boat so as not to fall into the water. After a while, Sam gave into his fatigue and dropped off to sleep. He was awakened by a loud noise. A boat approached and pulled along side.

The Coast Guard was surveilling the area after the storm, when they spotted Sam and pulled him to safety, covering him with a blanket to stop the shivering.

"You must look for Jeanne," Sam cried. "I can't-- I tried-- I can't find her."

"Don't worry. We'll find her," the officer said kindly.

Sam vomited the water he had ingested. After a shot of bourbon, he started to regain some strength. The Coast Guard circled the water in all directions, looking for some sign of life. Seeing nothing, they made an SOS call to the local authorities, where arrangements were made for a helicopter search of the area. Sam could hear the helicopter overhead as he was transported to the hospital. There was no sign of Jeanne. After a few hours, the futile search was called off.

Sam was examined at the hospital. He did not appear to have sustained any injury. The doctors advised him to remain in the hospital overnight for observation. Sedated, he slept through the night.

The next day, the police and the Coast Guard conducted an additional search of the area where the sailboat was discovered. Jeanne's body had not been found. The boat was towed to the police station for further examination.

-7-

Sara, Sam and Jeanne's daughter, arrived in Aruba and offered comfort to her father. After a week, they completed the bureaucratic paper work and returned home grief stricken. Sam was inconsolable. He slumped into a depressed state. He stopped eating and sleeping. He even stopped bathing and took to wearing the same clothes without changing. Sam slept on the couch in the living room, not able to stand the thought of sleeping in their bed. Sara could not comfort her father. She was concerned with his behavior and was too distraught to leave. But leave she must. Her family needed her. There were two young children to consider.

He refused to go home with her. "I need to be here in case they find Mom," he cried emphatically. But he promised to see his doctor.

As the weeks passed, Sam's friends tried to pull him out of his despair. George, Sam's best friend, came every day and sat with him. There was very little conversation. George talked. Sam didn't answer or at best occasionally grunted a one word response to a question. The silence was overwhelming.

When George left, Sam spent the day staring at the television screen, not seeing any programs. Ann, George's wife, brought him food and did his laundry. She gave him paper plates since Sam didn't wash the dishes. He picked at the food so generously provided, throwing most of it in the garbage. He lost twenty pounds and had grown a gray shaggy beard which added ten years to his appearance. His gaunt, pale face made Sam look old and haggard. His eyes and voice lacked emotion.

-8-

George and Ann decided to make Sam more independent. They forced him to fend for himself and provide his own nourishment. George shortened his visits. After several months Sam started to heal. George's visits were sparse, but he still called and tried to persuade him to become part of a group. Sam became morose and realized he was in need of human company. Out of desperation, Sam finally agreed to go to a meeting of widows and widowers bereavement group.

He entered the room timidly, looking around self-consciously. The room was filled with beige bridge chairs facing a podium. There was a mix of men and women milling around, drinking coffee, while engrossed in conversation. They all wore name tags.

Molly Browner, a nice looking plump woman with short gray hair and pretty eyes to match, was a widow for almost a year and a regular at these meetings. She greeted Sam. "Hello! My name is Molly Browner. Welcome."

"Hello, Sam Golden," he stammered.

"Come get a cup of coffee. We always have nice cake," she said with a smile. She took his arm and led him to the refreshment table, chattering as they walked.

Pouring Sam a cup of coffee, Molly told him about how helpful the group had been for her. "I was so lonely after Harry died," she said. "My friends didn't understand what I was going through. I needed people in the same situation as me. I found that here. I've made many new friends."

Sam told Molly how deserted he felt. He found it very easy to talk to her, as if they knew each other. They exchanged basic family information -- children, grandchildren, home. The usual banter of two strangers meeting.

The meeting started and the agenda was composed of individual stories of the members and how they were dealing, or not dealing, with the absence of their spouse or significant other. Sam saw himself in their stories.

He didn't mingle after the meeting, even though several people introduced themselves, trying to make him feel welcome. He started to leave and Molly came over to say good-night. "I hope you'll come again next week," she said handing him a piece of paper. "Here's my phone number in case you feel like talking."

"Goodnight. Thanks," he muttered and escaped.

Sam came home, collapsed on his reclining chair in the den, and had himself a good cry. His body was wracked with sobs. He thought how could I have had such a good time? My Jeanne is dead, and I was laughing and talking and drinking coffee. He was beside himself with mixed emotions.

The ringing of the telephone broke the spell. Wiping his tear-stained face, he picked up the phone.

"Hi Daddy," Sara said. "Are you all right? You sound peculiar."

"I'm-m uh fine. I was dozing on the chair when you called."

"Why didn't you call me back? I called before and when there was no answer, I left a message. Where were you?"

"Uh, I was out."

"Out! You? You never go out in the evening. Are you sure you're O.K.?"

"I went to a meeting of widows and widowers over at the Y."

"Good job. I'm so happy that you're finally getting around. Did you have a good time? Did you meet any nice people?"

"Sara, I really had a good evening. Everyone was nice and the agenda dealt with people like me. But I feel so sad. I miss Mom very much."

"I know. So do I. But you should go back again. You should, you know."

"I guess so. I'll think about it. How are Bob and the children?"

"All's well. I have to go now. Glad to hear you're coming out of your shell. When are you going to visit us?"

"Soon, I promise. Good-night! Love to all."

"Good-night, Daddy!" There was a tear in her voice.

*

Sam started to go out and about. He would meet George for coffee a few mornings in Starbucks and would remain when some men they knew joined them. Most afternoons, however, he could be found back in front of the TV. He was surprised to find himself waiting for Thursday to roll around.

Thursday evening, promptly at 7 o'clock, he walked into Room 10 of the Y, where the group would be meeting. Some people were already there. He almost lost his nerve, but decided to be brave, and hesitatingly shuffled in. An attractive woman, with blonde hair cascading to her shoulders, came towards him. She was wearing a red pants suit with a V-necked white blouse, and a pearl choker at her neck.

"Hello," she said smiling with an outstretched hand. "I'm Sylvia Lerner." *How good looking he is she thought.*

"Hello. Sam Golden, here," he said shaking her hand.

"I'm glad to meet you. Come on in. Join the bunch," she said, still holding onto his hand. She directed him to a group of people and introduced him.

"This is Sam Golden," Sylvia said reluctantly letting go of his hand.

"Hi. I'm Dave Williams," Dave said shaking Sam's hand.

"I'm also Sam. But Morris is my last name."

"Dotty Green," nodded the woman in the blue pants suit.

He met several more people as they came in. Sylvia, still at his side, was directing his attention. He glanced around the room looking for Molly to no avail. The meeting was called to order and everyone took their seat; Sylvia sat next to Sam.

During the coffee hour Molly came over, smiled, and said "Hi Sam. Nice to see you! Glad you could come."

His face brightened and he gave a big smile. "Molly, I looked for you. Did you just get here?"

"I was a little late. I had to do an errand, but I made it."

Sylvia felt left out and tried to reposition Sam to face her. Molly, being polite, included Sylvia in the conversation. Alas, Sam's attention was towards Molly. He felt awkward around Sylvia as she was preening him, fixing his hair, and caressing his arm; her conversation was about herself. Annoyed, Sam thought, *what a pest she is. I did this. I did that. I am wonderful. What a pest she is.*

People started to leave as the evening was coming to an end. Sylvia asked, "Sam would you be kind enough to drive me home? I only live a few blocks from here. I walked here, but it being so late I'm afraid to walk alone."

Sam hesitated and felt he had no choice but to agree.

"Good-night," Molly said as she walked towards her car. "See you soon."

He left Sylvia off at her house and went home, feeling let down. He didn't have a meaningful conversation and didn't have a chance to enjoy Molly's company. "I'll call her," he said emphatically.

-9-

Meanwhile, Sylvia decided to call Sam first thing in the morning and invite him for dinner. *We'll eat by candlelight and he'll get to know me. I'll have to move fast. He was* looking *at Molly, although I don't know why. She's fat and not classy.* "Can't hold a candle to me," she laughed out loud in the empty room. "I'll win him in a minute." She went to sleep planning what outfit she would wear.

The following morning the phone woke Sam.

"Hi Sammy! Did I wake you?" Sylvia cooed.

"I was getting up anyway," he answered sleepily.

"Sammy, how about coming for dinner tonight? I make a mean roast chicken and dumplings."

Sam hesitated and said, "Sorry, I'm busy. We'll have to make it another time."

"How about tomorrow?" she asked.

Not knowing what to say and being a bad liar, he said "O.K."

"Good. See you at six. You know where I live."

I'll have to think of an excuse to leave early, he thought, hanging up the phone. Before he had a chance to think, he called Molly Browner.

"Good morning," Sam said.

"Hi and how are you?" Molly answered.

Without delay, before he lost his nerve, he said "Molly, how about going to a movie with me tonight?" He held his breath, waiting for her reply.

"Sure," she said. "I'm dying to see Harry Potter. I know it's a kids' movie ... is it O.K. with you?"

"You bet," he said not really knowing who Harry Potter was. "I'll check the paper for the time and call you later."

"Bye, bye," Molly said.

-10-

Dr. Gonzalez, head of the trauma division of the Central Hospital of Caracas, Venezuela, took the pulse of the mystery woman. While holding her hand and counting the beats, his mind wandered. He was experienced and therefore could still be proficient at his task. He continued to hold her hand after he mentally recorded the pulse rate of 68. *It's low but within normal limits.* She's been in a coma for more than three months and he wanted to give her some physical connection. Being a compassionate man he felt her aloneness. *To be without any known family or friends is very sad,* he thought. The starkness of the room and the muted gray color added no joy. There had been an attempt by the nursing staff to brighten the room, but barely. They had brought flowers left by other patients and put them on the stand next to her bed. The quiet was deafening, just the periodic swish of the monitor, the soft murmurs and occasional foot steps of the staff.

Dr. Delgado, at Dr. Gonzalez' request, had come in as a consultant. He proceeded to do a cursory examination; listening to her heart and lungs, checking her eye grounds to ascertain any response. There was none. Dr. Delgado described his findings to Dr. Gonzalez. "This very thin woman, with a peaceful expression, appears to be sleeping. She is very pretty although wan with a pallid color and dark circles under her eyes." He noted that the white bed linens surrounding her made her appear even more colorless." The intravenous feedings are not enough to add weight to this frail body," Dr. Delgado concurred with Dr. Gonzalez.

Dr. Gonzalez added, "It is amazing that her physical condition steadily improves." He lifted her extremities to try to elicit any spontaneous movement. Her arms and legs were spindle- like, lifeless and dead weight. The doctors decided to add more calories to her feedings and to concur again in a week.

The nurses called her Fulana, Spanish for Jane Doe. Dr. Gonzalez said to the nurse in the room, "Still no response," gently lowering the patient's legs. "I can't figure why she doesn't come out of the coma. The neurological tests have come back with negative results. The neurologist is as baffled as I am."

"The hypothermia and large amount of water she ingested must be the culprit," the nurse answered as she smoothed the blanket. "Her vital signs are good as are her breath sounds. Blood pressure is low but certainly not alarmingly so. 95/60 for a woman in her condition is O.K.," Nurse Diaz reported.

"I would so like to bring her out of the coma," the good doctor said sadly. "Maybe she has had a hard life and really doesn't want to continue. We know nothing about her, which makes the treatment so much more difficult," Maria Diaz said as she fluffed the pillows and fixed Fulana's hair. Maria believed that even if someone was very ill that person should be neat and clean. She always tried to keep her patients looking as well as possible.

"She must have come from somewhere," the doctor said, "But from where and from how far?" There were no signs of a wreckage. A person doesn't just appear out of the water like Aphrodite, goddess of love, who sprung from the foam in the sea."

Maria reported, "The local fisherman who picked her out of the water said that her color was bluish. He wrapped her in blankets and tried to keep her warm. It seems as if she was in the water for a long time, whatever a long time means. He said that he put her on her stomach and hit her back trying to get her to vomit the water, which she did."

They kept trying to see whether they had missed an important piece of the puzzle. Dr. Gonzalez picked up the story and said, "She was discovered outside of the entrance to the emergency room. At the ER, they told me that they had suctioned large amounts of water out of the patient, and she appeared to be hypothermic. I had her stomach pumped to rid her body of the water. Her BP was dangerously low, 60/40, as was her body temperature of 12c. Her breath sounds were slight with rales in her lungs. I hoped that she would not have pneumonia as well as any additional major problems. Her heart seemed strong in spite of what occurred. She was immediately packed in warm water soaks, which helped to raise the temperature. In a few days, the IV saline drip, enhanced with caloric additives, brought her vital signs to the lower limits of normal. "Good, she is a strong lady."

Nurse Diaz said, "Social Services has contacted local authorities and those of nearby Curacao, to see if there is a missing person report to fit the description of our Fulana. They also made contact with shipping lines that have been in the area as well as private charter boats. There doesn't seem to be any record of this lady. She was admitted as Fulana and remains as such."

-11-

The days passed uneventfully for the mystery woman. There was very little change in her physical condition. Blood pressure, vital signs, breath sounds were still low but within the lower ranges of normal. Dr. Gonzalez checked her daily and worried about the lack of improvement, and sometimes checked her again before he went home. He had no family, and he was in no rush. To know this woman, to make her well, became an obsession.

One evening, five and one-half months after admission, the patient blinked her eyes and moved her fingers. There was no one in the room to see this. However, the slight motion activated the monitor and the evening nurse, Senora Cruz, ran into the room. No movement. The patient had slipped back into the coma-like sleep.

The next day while Dr. Gonzalez was reading the chart at the nurses' station, the beeping from the monitors alerted him to some activity in the room. He ran in to find Fulana awake, looking around. "Buenas dias, Senorita. Mi nombre es Doctor Gonzalez."

The woman looked bewildered. She didn't look Spanish. She had a light complexion, blue eyes, and blonde hair, which had been colored but was now mostly gray. He continued slowly in English. "You are in a hospital. You have been very ill."

She tried to reach her throat, trying to remove the tube.

Dr. Gonzalez took her hand away, gently. "You are on a ventilator to help you breathe. We will watch you for another few hours and if you're still alert, I will remove it."

Her glazed eyes were wild with fright, as she didn't seem to understand what he was saying.

"Just relax," he said squeezing her hand trying to reassure her.

She calmed down, holding on to his hand, and finally slept.

*

As the week progressed, there was a miraculous turn around. She was removed from all equipment; ventilator, intra-venous tubes, and catheter. Her blood pressure rose to 110/70, her lung capacity was at 75%, and she started to eat soft, solid food.

Dr. Gonzalez stopped in every evening and engaged her in small talk, entertaining her with interesting occurrences of his day. After a few days she started to talk to him, hesitatingly, in incomplete sentences.

He told her how she was found and brought to the hospital. When he questioned her, "Senora, can you remember your name or where you live? You don't look Spanish. You speak English and sound like an American. Does this ring a bell?" She shook her head, no, with tears in her eyes.

"Don't worry. It will come," he said. He tried to gain her trust. He felt if she could be less anxious, she might start to remember.

The nurses continued to bring her left over flowers in an attempt to put some color into the room. She was now on a chair, and with the help of the physical therapist she started to walk. Her speech improved with the support of the speech therapist.

Questions about her identity remained unanswered. "I can't remember anything," she cried with tears running down her cheeks. "I'm trying," she said weakly.

She was assured by the staff that her memory would return, although as time passed, they were not so sure. The mystery woman became their pet. The patient was quite pleasant and tried hard to get well. She was cooperative and listened to the nurses, trying to help them as much as she could. They gave her a name, Marguerite. It seemed to fit her pleasant disposition. The evening nurses spent their breaks telling her about their own lives.

Senora Cruz said, "Since we are friends, call me Anna." She told Marguerite about her three children, Manuel, Anna, and Ramon, and how well they did in school. "Marguerite, how far did you go in school? Did you graduate from high school?"

She tried hard to remember. "I really don't know."

Senorita Rojo regaled her with stories of her experiences as a nurse, treating patients with difficult personalities. They both laughed when Julia Rojo told how she had to handle the patient who pinched her every time she walked by his bed.

Dr.Gonzalez grew fonder of Marguerite. He decided she needed a change of scenery and invited her to dinner on Saturday night. He took her to a small restaurant down the street from the hospital in a wheelchair, as he was afraid her first outing would be too much for her.

They settled in and when the waiter handed them their menus, she said surprisingly, "I can't read the menu."

"That's because it's in Spanish," the good doctor laughed. "What do you like to eat? Meat, fish, chicken?"

"I don't know," she said quietly, ashamed that she knew nothing about herself.

"No problema. I will order for us. Senor," he motioned to the waiter, "dos ensaladas, dos arroz con pollo, y dos cafe con leche. Gracias! I have ordered salads, chicken and rice and coffee. The food is very good here and their coffee the best. By the way, call me Ramon. Dr. Gonzalez is much too formal."

She appeared fragile, sitting in the large high backed wooden chair, almost as if she would disappear. She was very nervous and played with her napkin and the silverware in repetitive movements, although she ate most of the meal.

"The coffee is wonderful," she said with a smile. "Hot and strong! I'm having a good time. Thank you for being so nice to me."

"De nada, don't mention it," Ramon replied. Unfortunately we must go back. You shouldn't be out so long on your first trip. We'll do it again."

They returned to the hospital and Marguerite who was weak, pale and breathless, fell asleep immediately.

*

Plans were made to discharge Marguerite, as there was no longer a reason to keep her in the hospital. She would require outpatient care with the physical and speech therapists, and check-ups from the medical doctor. The social worker secured her a room in a house where the owner, a retired nurse, took care of adults with disabilities. Since she had no money, the government would pay her expenses for at least ninety days.

The big day arrived all too quickly. The nurses, doctors, and attendants from the forth floor of the hospital, gathered to say good-bye. It had been more than six months since she was first brought in. They feted her with a chocolate cake filled with cherries and covered in whipped cream. The top of the cake was decorated with flowers and had Bueno Suerte, Good-Luck, in Spanish written across it. They had chipped in and bought her three outfits; two pants, a skirt, and three blouses. Marguerite's hair was cut, framing her face in soft gray curls, and her nails were manicured with light pink polish. The hairdresser gave her services as a gift. Social services provided shoes, a jacket, underwear, and toiletries. Anna Cruz gave her a slightly used handbag.

Marguerite was overwhelmed at the kindness provided to her. She still couldn't remember her past, but with her fighting spirit she concentrated on the present. Despite her circumstances, she was enjoying her newly found friends.

-12-

Sam's friendship with Molly and Sylvia grew day by day. He enjoyed Molly's company. They had much in common, spending hours prowling the art museums. The Whitney and the Frick were favorites, and lunch at Sarafays' in the Whitney was a must. The chocolate cake and latte's completed their afternoons. They attended the special exhibits at the Metropolitan Museum of Art. Gauguin and Degas were outstanding and they discussed them at length.

"I love the Tahitian women that Gauguin paints," Molly said during lunch in the cafeteria of the museum. "His colors are brilliant."

"Their figures could be a little sexier, don't you think? His native women are a little chunky," Sam laughed.

"A little chunky like me, only not so bland" she laughed.

Sam added, "But seriously the character of their faces are very sensual, indicative of Island woman, as you are my dear."

Molly blushed, enjoying the complement.

*

During dinner a few weeks later, they still continued comparisons of the exhibit with much interest. They talked about Degas' ballerinas. "The famous sculpture of the ballerina in her tutu is magnificent," Molly said. "The way that Degas captures her stance is so real. The positions of his ballerinas in his paintings, makes them appear to be dancing right off the canvas."

"This exhibit reminds me of Jeanne. She loved Degas. She read books about his life and we even traveled to the National Gallery in Washington, D.C. to see his work." A lump gathered in Sam's throat as he remembered that episode of their life. He still missed Jeanne.

Molly was sympathetic. "My Harry didn't care for art museums. I went with my friends." Purposely changing the subject she said, "Sam, we must start going to some art lectures at the Met. You would enjoy them."

Grateful for the interruption, he said, "Fine. Sure"

Having the same interests helped them become a couple. They loved Central Park. They would walk through the park, or sit on a bench, people-watching. Sometimes they would wander to the lake, have coffee at the boathouse, and watch the swans and the people in the rowboats.

They also enjoyed the movies. Many an afternoon was spent seeing a good film. Foreign films at the art theaters were their forte. They had no sexual relationship. It was rather a very friendly one, giving both a warm feeling.

Sylvia, on the other hand, introduced life, fun, and silliness into Sam's life. Her mood was always up, and she was on the go. "Let's go to Little Italy in the village for pastries at Ferrara," she would say on the spur of the moment, or "I hear there's a good dance band at Roseland. We must go," she would coo. She was a good dancer, and they went often to the senior center's monthly dances.

"I can't keep up with you," Sam said more than once, trying to put some distance between them. Sylvia still clung tightly as she danced.

"Sure you can. We'll sit out some of the fast numbers and concentrate on the slow ones. More romantic anyway! By the way, when are we going away for the weekend? We need some time alone concentrating on the bedroom," Sylvia winked.

Sam's face turned bright red and his eyes opened wide with embarrassment. *In my whole life I never met such a forward woman,* he thought, although the idea of a weekend was planted in his subconscious.

One day Sylvia called and said, "Pack your bags-- we're going to Cape Cod. I've booked a room for us at a bed and breakfast overlooking the Atlantic. It's off- season so the place should be empty. We can sunbathe, go clamming, take a stroll on the beach, and enjoy a picnic lunch near sweeping sand dunes hidden from anyone' view."

"Wait a minute," Sam stammered.

"No waits," she interrupted. "Now is the time. We'll leave Friday morning *early* and come back Sunday *late*. Pick me up at 8 o'clock. See ya," she purred in a low voice, as she hung up.

Sam remained holding the receiver, palms sweating. "A weekend," he said aloud. "How?" Putting the phone down he thought, *how can I go? How will I look? No woman other than Jeanne has seen me naked in years. Jeanne and I were good together. We knew each other. But, another woman? I'm an old man and look like one. My belly is big, my behind is wrinkled, my legs are spindly and oh my God... Will it work?* He panicked. He had to sit down. His face was flushed, heart beating, hands shaking. He got up and rushed to the kitchen for a glass of water. He needed the drink to revive himself.

He sat back down, took some deep breaths and slowly started to relax. *Maybe it will be O.K. We'll be out all day and at night the lights will be out. Wouldn't it be great if I can still do it? Maybe! Sylvia's not so young either, although in better shape.* "More experienced too, I'll bet," he chuckled. "I'm such a square."

He started to yawn, went to bed and dreamed of the wonderful time he and Sylvia would have. In the morning he said, "I'll go. What can happen? It won't be good, so she'll stop calling."

In the morning, Sam called his daughter. "Hi honey, how's the family?"

"Good Dad. Is everything all right? I spoke to you yesterday."

"I just wanted to tell you that I'm going away for the weekend. We're going to the Cape."

"Great," she answered. "Dad, you said we. Who are you going with?"

"Your old man is spending a few days with a female friend. How do you like that? Me an old guy-- a tete- a- tete."

Sara was floored. She didn't answer immediately. A few seconds passed, and she said slowly, "A woman? How well do you know this person? What are you getting yourself into?"

Disappointed, Sam said, "Well enough. I thought that you'd be happy for me. You're always pushing me to go out and not sit home alone." There was silence for a moment and Sam continued, "Honey, no one can replace your Mother. She will always be in my heart."

Realizing what she must have sounded like, she said sheepishly, "Sorry Daddy. I hope you have a good time with your friend. But be careful and call me when you get home. Bye."

Hanging up the telephone, Sam rethought his decision to go and considered canceling. *Maybe I'm making a mistake. Maybe it's too early. Maybe Sylvia is too much of a woman for me. She's so different from Jeanne.*

With that thought on his mind, the phone rang. It was Sylvia. "Good morning glory. My clothes are packed and I can't wait."

"Me too," Sam stammered.

-13-

Molly called Sam. "Sam, *Casablanca* is playing at the Fine Arts Theatre. Wanna go?"

"Uh, I'm busy," he stammered. "Can we make it another night?"

"Sure. How about Saturday?"

Swallowing hard, he blurted, "I'm going away for the weekend. I'll be back on Sunday."

"Did you just decide? You didn't mention it the other night."

"I wasn't sure I was going. That's why I didn't say anything. I'm going to the Cape."

"Have a good time. Call me when you get back." Molly wondered who he was going with. *I wish I had nerve to ask, but don't want to pry,* she thought. *Maybe he's going with his daughter. I wish I was going with them.* "Oh well, another lonely weekend," she sighed, turning on the T.V.

*

Friday morning found Sam at Sylvia's. He barely had stopped the car when she was out of the door. "Sam, come help me with my bag."

"Here I come."

The ride to the Cape was pleasant. Sylvia did most of the talking leaving Sam free to concentrate on the road. "The trees are gorgeous this time of year," Sylvia said. "Reds, oranges, yellows; they cover the ground like a multi-colored carpet... Look at all of these cars... Where are all of these people going?... Sam, look at that gorgeous church and the beautiful steeple."

"Uh, huh."

They crawled through morning traffic on Rte. 95 through New Haven at a snail's pace.

The traffic broke as they left the city. Sylvia continued her babbling.

"Finally on our way again! Honey, I called my son to tell him we were going away. He was pleased."

"Uh huh!"

As they entered Massachusetts, going further into New England, the trees became sparse. She looked at Sam, batted her eyelashes and said, "Honey, you know I like spring better than fall. A new beginning, instead of a closing -- just like us."

Sam coughed, *honey,* and wondered what "us" meant to her. *To me there is no us,* he thought. He took a deep breath and was suddenly aware of the fruity smell from Sylvia's fragrance. He smiled.

"I'm hungry," Sam said at noon time. "Let's stop at the next exit."

While walking into the Cracker Barrel Restaurant and General Store, Sam noticed a friend of his daughter. "Oh, no," he said a frown crossing his face. He ducked and hid behind the jam and jelly counter, while Sylvia went to leave their name at the restaurant.

Why am I hiding like a child, Sam pondered? Am I ashamed to be here? Who is Michelle to me, he thought, although he still didn't go out to greet her. He played with the jars and pretended to be studying the apple butter.

"Golden, your table is ready," the voice on the speaker announced.

"Sam," Sylvia hollered.

The sound of his name shook him out of his reverie. He looked around the display counter, and not seeing Michelle, left his hiding place. "The coast is clear," he mumbled as he started into the restaurant to join Sylvia.

"Hey, Mr. Golden – Hello! It's Michelle, Sara's friend," Michelle said as she headed toward him. "I heard your name on the loudspeaker but didn't associate it with you. What a surprise. How ya been?"

"Uh, fine, great. I didn't see you when we came in," he said guiltily.

"I'm on my way to the Cape to visit my aunt -- it's her birthday -- sixty-five years old, I can't believe it." She glanced at Sylvia." Where are you going?" Michelle asked, without taking a breath

"I'm Sylvia Lerner," Sylvia said, wrapping her arm possessively around Sam's.

"Hi," Michelle said.

"We're going to the Cape too," Sylvia said in a firm voice. "Staying in a quaint bed and breakfast."

A bright blush framed Sam's face. His eyes roamed the area, ignoring direct contact with Michelle.

"Mr. Golden, does Sara know you're here?" Michelle asked ignoring

Sylvia. "I spoke to her before I left and she didn't say anything. We're very close, you know."

"I guess she forgot," Sam said, as he guided Sylvia towards the restaurant. "Michelle, nice seeing you, but we have to get our table. Have a nice party." He practically pushed Sylvia.

"Slow down, Sam," Sylvia said as the hostess led them to their table.

Michelle continued staring at them as she contemplated Sam's behavior. *It's not like him to ignore me. He's always so friendly. After all, he knows me for so many years. He seemed so uncomfortable. What's up with him? And her, she's so pushy holding him like he'll run away. I'll have to call Sara when I get home.*

-14-

Sam and Sylvia checked into the Inn, and were shown to their suite. A four-poster bed, with a ruffled canopy in a print of large white and yellow flowers, was on the far wall. Framed pictures of a variety of flowers, in all colors, surrounded the triple dresser. The room was furnished quietly in a colonial motif.

The sitting section of the suite had a small light blue striped settee, wing backed chairs covered in a darker shade of blue with little white flowers. There were duplicate old fashioned lamps of rose colored glass globes. A small coffee table sat in front of the sofa. A slight breeze rippled the lace curtains. The stone fireplace completed the room.

The room looked out onto the ocean. The pounding sound of the waves against the rocks could be heard through the open windows. A bottle of wine in a bucket, with two wine glasses stood on the table.

"Wow," Sam said when he entered the suite. "It's gorgeous."

Sylvia smiled as she opened the wine. "A toast to a great weekend," she said filling each glass. They clinked glasses and sipped zinfandel.

"Let's unpack later," Sylvia said, making the first move, as she approached Sam. Her hands framed his face as she kissed him squarely on the lips. He responded and caressed her. They soon headed for the bed. He breathed in her familiar fragrance as she unbuttoned his shirt and opened the belt on his trousers. Sam tried to take her sweater off but was clumsy and fumbled with it trying to get it over her head. She helped him as he mumbled hesitatingly, "I've not been with another woman since Jeanne."

"Don't worry. Let nature take its course," Sylvia replied in a voice husky with emotion.

And it did. They embraced, kissed, hugged, explored, and made love slowly and easily; not with the passion of twenty year olds, but satisfying to them both. Sam gave a contented sigh, and said, "I'm sixty-six years old but today I feel like a young man."

"Compliments to me?" Sylvia cooed coquettishly.

He laughed, yawned and was soon lightly snoring, in a deep sleep.

I've got him now, Sylvia thought cuddling next to Sam. *Molly is history. Lead a man into a bed and he's yours.*

They took a walk after a delicious dinner in the old fashioned paneled dining room, in front of a wood burning fire. The town was quiet. The sky in full bloom, with a bright shining waning moon. The couple returned to their room drowsy from the day's events.

*

They spent the next day at the beach warmed and relaxed by the bright autumn sun. While Sam dozed in a chaise underneath a beach umbrella, he remembered the last day he spent with Jeanne. They were on the beach in Aruba. In his dream he heard their conversation.

"This is a wonderful idea you had," Jeanne said to Sam.

"Isn't it though?" he laughed.

He saw her laughing face and blue eyes sparkling like stars in the sky. He smelled the Shalimar that was her trademark perfume.

"Let's go for a swim," she said running into the ocean.

He followed yelling, "Wait for me."

They dove into the waves and came up together.

"I feel like a young man," Sam sputtered with water splashing in his face and mouth.

"You are a young man," Jeanne responded pushing the wet hair away from her face. "We have a lot of years together. Let's enjoy them."

They held hands and jumped up and down with the waves.

"Sam, Sam, wake up," Sylvia shook him. "You're twisting and turning. What's the matter?"

Still half asleep, and holding his hands out, he said, "Jeanne, Jeanne."

Sylvia shook him again. "It's me Sylvia. Jeanne's dead."

He opened his eyes wide and looked straight at her not able to speak. He felt as if he had been slapped across the face.

"No, no. She's alive somewhere. I know it."

Later when he was composed, Sam apologized for his outburst.

"I'm sorry how I acted, Syl. I had a dream and couldn't shake it. It was so real."

"It's O.K.," she whispered. "It's O.K." She smoothed his forehead with the back of her hand.

The weekend progressed pleasantly. The next day it rained, and they went to a movie in the afternoon. They saw a new version of Sabrina.

They agreed, "Without Audrey Hepburn and Humphrey Bogart it just wasn't the same." It added to the gloom of the day and the scene from yesterday.

That night they slept together in the large comfortable bed without any real contact.

She tried; he politely refused.

"I'm tired," he said. "We've had a long day."

When he dropped her off at her house, and brought in her suitcase, he apologized again, as he gave her a peck on the lips.

"We'll do it again," she said.

*

The phone was ringing as Sam opened the door to his house.

"Hi Dad! When did you get home? Did you have a good time? How was the weather?"

"Sara, you still talk without taking a breath. You exhaust me just listening to you."

"Sorry, Dad, but don't evade the questions."

"It was fine. I had a good time. It rained. How are Bob, Brianna and Jeremy?"

"Good, good. Michelle called and said she saw you and your friend. She said you looked good but *she* looked like a floozy. Is she? Lots of makeup and smelled like a flower, she continued without missing a beat.

"Sara, don't start," Sam said in a weary voice. "Sylvia is a very nice woman."

"Michelle also said that *that* woman held on to you for dear life; as if you might run away," Sara rambled on.

Grinning, Sam admitted, "Well maybe she's a little pushy." He was finally able to laugh.

-15-

Sam's mind wandered as he unpacked his clothes from the weekend. "Well I'll be damned," he said surprising himself when he heard his voice. "Maybe she is alive?" He stopped his task and sat down on the bed, thinking about his outburst the other day when Sylvia said Jeanne was dead. I spoke without thinking. Maybe that was the sign I was waiting for. My brain always told me she was dead; my heart felt different.

He immediately got out the yellow pages and looked for Private Investigators. He had hired one right after the accident, to no avail. Perhaps now is the right time. He called the first listing in the column, AAA Private Investigation.

"AAA Private Investigation, Jeffrey Atlas speaking."

"Mr. Atlas, my name is Sam Golden. I need to make an appointment to speak to you."

"Ten tomorrow morning! O.K., Mr. Golden.?"

"Absolutely! See you then."

*

After the introductions, Sam outlined his needs in just a few short sentences. "My wife and I were in a boat accident almost a year ago in Aruba. She was never found. I want to find her. Can you help me?"

"I'll need the details of the accident, the follow-up and a copy of the accident reports. I'll let you know when I'm done with them."

They shook hands and Sam left feeling a weight lifted from his chest. He decided to keep this a secret because he thought that everyone would pity him and his obsession.

A few days after he gave Mr. Atlas the requested material and a recent picture and description of his wife, Sam and Jeff, as the P.I. wanted to be called, agreed on a fee and the case was opened. Jeff promised weekly reports and immediate contact should something of importance occur.

The process began with a search of the internet. Jeff looked up missing persons found in each of the Caribbean Islands. He batted zero. No one fitting the description of Jeanne Golden could be found. He checked every website he could think of. He discussed the case with some private eyes that he used from time to time. He circulated her picture among his colleagues. There was reciprocity among them and they often did this in the event that someone hired another private investigator to either locate somebody or to investigate someone's past. Another dead end! He spoke with his police contacts in the Caribbean area. No one came close. His reports to Sam were discouraging.

"Don't give up," Sam appealed. "I can afford another month or two. Please continue."

"I'm going to fly to Aruba to see for myself," Jeff said.

"Good. Good."

-16-

Arriving in Aruba, Jeff immediately went to the hospital armed with his flyer, a picture of Jeanne and identifying information concerning her. Jeff showed Jeanne's picture to hotel personnel, restaurant and nightclub workers, anyone he could think of. He combed the beach looking at the tourists. He went to the gambling casinos at different hours; days, evenings and nights, and spoke with the croupiers and entertainers. No one recognized her. No one remembered seeing her.

Mike O'Hara, the local police chief and Jeff's friend said, "Why don't you go to Curacao to look? A boat taking tourists goes once a day."

"Great idea," Jeff said "Thanks pal."

He repeated the same pattern of searching on the neighboring island of Curacao, with no results. No one had seen a woman fitting the description; a blonde, blue eyed woman, about five foot five, with a slim build weighing approximately one-hundred and thirty pounds. She usually wore her hair back from her face. Another dead end!

While having a cold beer in a local bar in town, he finally decided he would go home. He was wasting Mr. Golden's money and accomplishing nothing. It was early afternoon and the bar was almost empty; just a few shapeless characters quietly drinking. The lights were low and the place appeared shoddy. The faded red leatherette on some of the stools were cracked and in need of attention. The radio played an old Billie Holliday song. The constant whirr of the overhead fans and the depressing picture of the bar somehow lulled Jeff into a sad mood. He told his story to the bartender who suggested a trip to Caracas. "It's not far. I know it's a big city, but, you never know."

"I'm interested," Jeff said. "I never thought about Caracas. I concentrated on the islands. Thank you very much. I owe you," he said shaking Joe the bartenders' hand.

Jeff made a phone call to Sam, apprising him of his plans. Sam was appreciative of the new course of action. "Better than quitting," he said.

-17-

Sam spent a lot of time in his house, immersed in the scheme to locate Jeanne. He still didn't discuss it with anyone. He bought himself a computer and had it installed immediately. The deal included some lessons. After a few futile attempts to use it, and some additional lessons, he was able to master the internet. He was determined and used the days looking for any avenues he could find which would help him locate a missing person. His missing person!

Sylvia was breaking down the telephone asking him where he was and why he was staying home. "Sam, what's wrong? ... I miss you... Are you sick? ... You can tell me, I'll help you."

"Sylvia, nothing is wrong. I need some time to myself. Like the youngsters I have to find myself, and I need to do it alone. I'll call you soon."

She came to the house with a pot roast dinner. Then she came with a chicken dinner. "You have to eat." She tried the old adage, "the way to a man's heart is through his stomach." Nothing worked.

Sam was adamant about his plan. "Sylvia, enough," he shouted finally showing his anger at her pressuring him.

Molly called too, but she wasn't so pesty. "Hi Sam, it's me, Molly, in case you forgot."

"Sorry Molly. I'm going through some sort of crisis and I need to be alone. I promise to call you soon."

"Can I help you with your problems? I am a good listener. You can trust me."

"Thanks, but no. I have to handle this myself."

He isolated everyone and liked the solitude and the time spent with the computer. He lied to Sara, telling her how he was having a good time at the Center and promised her he would come to see her at the beginning of next month. She badgered him and threatened that if he didn't come to her, she would come to him.

"Dad, I haven't seen you for months. I don't live around the world, just a few hours away. Unless you are ill, you better come."

"I promise. I would come sooner but I'm busy fixing up some things in the house."

"D-a-d, you fixing? Since when? The only things you fixed were in the garden."

"Things change. People change. Sara don't worry. I'm fine," he said in a strong voice hiding the trembling that he felt.

"I have to see her," he said as he hung up the telephone.

Sam's best friend George, came to see him and tormented him into telling him what was wrong. Sworn to secrecy, Sam blurted out his mission.

"Don't laugh. I'm looking for Jeanne."

With his mouth open in awe, George said, "Sam are you crazy? How can she be alive? The Coast Guard searched for days. Flyers were posted. Get real."

"That's why I didn't tell anyone of my plan. I hired a private investigator who is looking for her now. Tell me, what have I got to lose? I feel as if I haven't had closure," he said weeping openly.

"O.K. O.K.," George said fighting back tears. "We've been friends for so many years. I feel for you. I really do. Can I help?"

With a new vitality, his mood brightened. "You are a computer whiz. Let's work together. Alone I don't seem to be accomplishing anything."

George immediately took over. He looked at Sam's list of websites and said, "Let me go over these and I'll get back to you tomorrow. I need some time to think."

"I was a fool to be afraid to share this with you. You're right. We go way back and I should have had confidence in our friendship."

-18-

Marguerite was enjoying her new life. She had no idea what her old one was like. From time to time, she looked in the mirror, and wondered about it. What did she do before? Where did she live? Did she have a family? She didn't even know her own name. But not allowing herself to wallow in self-pity, she would shake her head and say "Never mind," as if to throw away the demons.

She did volunteer work at the hospital where she went for physical therapy. She helped with other patients' also receiving treatment. Making sure that the packs were clean and hot became her job on Tuesday and Thursday mornings. While assisting the other ladies with dressing and undressing, she was able to get to know them. She hoped they would become friends and see each other in a social situation. She had no real friends.

A latent effect of the hypothermia was poor circulation, but due to the strenuous regime she was walking better and getting stronger. Warm packs were applied to her legs, followed by massage. The muscles had atrophied from lack of use. She also worked with light weights to increase her upper body strength. A stretching routine and riding the stationary bike completed her routine.

"Marguerite, you're a life saver," the therapist said. "You're such a big help. Your positive attitude is contagious."

She always blushed at the compliments, but secretly enjoyed them.

"I know you are short of dinero and wish we could get you a job here," Maria the head honcho said.

"I know. I have no working papers. Someday," she added with a sigh. "Living on public assistance is tough. This is the first time for me."

"How do you know that?" Maria asked startled. "Are you starting to remember?"

"I... I don't know. I still can't recall anything. I don't know where that came from."

"Don't worry sweetheart, it will come."

Dr. Gonzalez filled her time in the evening. He was in love and wanted to share all of his time with her.

"Mi amor, my love," he would say as a general greeting. "How are you today?"

"Bueno, bueno, mi amigo," she would answer in the few Spanish words she had picked up.

"Am I not more than an amigo?"

With a laugh, she said "Patience is a virtue. When did I learn this saying?" she blurted out. This is the second time I said something I was not aware of."

"See I told you it would come, and it will."

Marguerite was not sure that what she was feeling was love. It was certainly more than like, but love, she didn't know. Or was she afraid to commit.

"I do have feelings for you, Senor Doctor," she jested. "Seriously, I need some time," she said giving him a peck on the lips and a pat on his cheek.

Ramon gave her the royal tour of every nook and cranny in Caracas. It took them some time to do this as she wasn't strong enough to gallivant for a whole day.

"You must rest. Come let's have coffee," he would say in the afternoon. During their sojourn, they talked and were comfortable with each other. She heard about his family; two brothers, Juan and Cesar, and Angelina his sister. Both boys were married with two children each. Angelina a lawyer was still single. His grandfather lived with his parents.

"Mi abuelo, is my favorite. He has always been closer to me than my own father."

"I wonder if I knew my abuelo," she said sadly.

"It'll be my pleasure to make arrangements for us to have dinner with my family,"

Marguerite had promised to meet them. Ramon said with a grin. "They'll love you."

She knew he had never been married. He told her about several affairs that he had and he assured her he was currently unattached.

"I've been around, but with no one like you, Marguerite. My work at the hospital had been my life until you were brought there. How lucky I am. After sixty years, I finally found someone I truly care for. I hope the feeling becomes mutual."

"Ramon," Marguerite said one evening. I've been seriously thinking of trying to find my past. How could I go about doing that? I read that hypnotism could help. Do you think so?"

"I don't know," he said. "Mi amor, why dwell on the past? We have now."

"Maybe I could look at pictures of missing persons to jar my memory?" She continued without catching her breath, "I need to know. You want a commitment. How can I? Perhaps I have a husband and children. I must try."

Seeing how upset she was, Ramon assured Marguerite that he would try to find a way to help her relive her past. He would make inquiries in the hospital, with missing persons, and among his associates. "I'll help you. I promise."

-19-

"You're beautiful," Ramon said kissing Marguerite hello, when he picked her up to go to his family on Sunday.

"I'm so pale, I need some color, but thank you anyway kind sir," she laughed.

He should have seen me a few hours ago, she thought, how I changed my clothes three times, and spent the entire morning at the mirror. The red outfit-- too flashy; the black one-- too solemn. Maybe they won't like me in pants. I hope this black skirt and white blouse with red trim is suitable.

As they walked up to the porch, Marguerite said, "I'm shaking. I can hardly stand. Ramon, what will I talk about? I don't know anything. I can't even speak Spanish."

"Don't worry. They won't bite and they speak English, although my mother barely can."

As Ramon opened the door, she smelled the fragrant odor of food, and could hear talking and laughing. The family sounded so happy. "Buenos dias," Ramon said when they entered the living room.

Quiet filled the room. All talking stopped at once, as they looked at the couple.

Marguerite barely was able to say, "Good afternoon." Her mouth felt dry, like it was lined with cotton.

Ramon's brothers, Juan and Cesar, came forward to welcome them. They kissed Marguerite on the cheek. "Thank you," Ramon whispered to them as he gave them each a hug. Angelina, and Juan and Cesar's wives, Lupe and Carmen, and his parents remained at the dining room table. "Buenos Dias," they said in a pleasant manner although very formal.

The children ran to their uncle hugging him around his legs. He scooped them up as they giggled. "Meet my friend Marguerite," he said putting them down. They hid behind him each still holding a leg.

"Hello. I'm glad to meet you," Marguerite said getting some strength back in her voice. "What are your names?"

Maria, the oldest at ten, looked at her uncle for confidence and said shyly, "I'm Maria. This is my sister Anna. She's only six and this is my cousin Clara. She's five." Laughing, they ran back to their toys. Ramon took Marguerite into the dining room to meet the rest of the family.

"This is my mother, Frida, my father Ramon Senior, and my sister Angelina. We call her Lina, and my abuelo Jose." Ramon kissed his grandfather.

"Buenos dias," Marguerite said.

"Buenos tardes." They stood as they acknowledged her.

The room had a warm glow, with gold flocked wall paper and a gold and red flowered rug. The large oak table was covered with a white lace cloth. There were two large brass candle sticks with white candles glowing. The family was drinking red wine.

"A glass of sangria?" Juan asked.

"Sure," Ramon said. "Marguerite have one, it's delicious."

They both sipped the sweet drink poured from a pitcher filled with oranges, lemons and pineapples. The fruit would be eaten later with dessert.

Senora Gonzalez went into the kitchen and brought out a platter of roasted vegetables, with guacamole, and tortillas. "Have some," she said to the guest as she served her. The platter was placed in the center of the table.

Everyone sat down to this appetizer and soon were once again all talking.

Angelina, however, was quiet. She just sat and looked at Marguerite. "Where do you come from?" Being polite she thought, *did you have a husband back wherever you came from? And children?*

Startled, Marguerite stammered, "I don't know. I can't remember."

Can't remember? Lina reflected, thinking how convenient for someone to hide their past. "How did you come to Caracas?"

"Lina." Ramon said a little too loudly. "Enough."

"Mama, how about dinner?" Cesar said trying to clear the air.

Angelina did not shut up. "How do you know you don't have a husband back wherever you came from? And children?"

Marguerite, barely whispered, "I don't know. I have thought about it. I don't know." Ramon glared at his sister. She became quiet. The food was brought out by Senora Gonzalez, Lupe and Carmen. The platters overflowed with goodies; a pork roast, chicken with rice, enchiladas stuffed with meat, and an assortment of vegetables.

"This is a wonderful meal, Mrs. Gonzalez," Marguerite said.

"But you are hardly eating." Mrs. Gonzalez added more food to Marguerite's plate.

"I don't have a big appetite."

Carmen in a friendly manner said, "In this family you must eat at the Sunday dinner. It's expected."

The family tried to include Marguerite in the conversation. They made her feel welcome except for Angelina. She kept her distance and was quiet throughout the dinner.

I wonder if she really can't remember, she thought. Is she playing the poor soul to get my brother to feel sorry for her? I'll have to do a little investigating. Maybe she's a gold digger. After all he is a doctor with a sizable income.

The afternoon ended pleasantly. As they bid their good-byes they told Marguerite she must come again.

-20-

Jeff Atlas arrived at the Caracas airport on a hot muggy day. The humidity caused his shirt to cling to his body. He went directly to the Caracas Hilton, checked in, unpacked, showered and called Miguel Corrado. Mike O'Hara had connected him with this private investigator who was familiar with the city.

"He's a gem. Right on the money, knows everyone," Mike said about Corrado.

Over lunch in the hotel, Jeff filled Miguel in on the details of his search. "The husband is desperate to find out whether his wife is alive."

"I read the police report you faxed," Miguel said. "How could she be alive? No one could swim that far to land. It's impossible."

"Any chance that a private fishing boat picked her up?"

"I spoke to my friends at the police station. There was no report, official or unofficial, about any person being picked up from the sea. I spoke to some local fishermen, in the bars near the dock and on the dock itself. No one remembers anything about a questionable individual. Lo siento amigo."

Jeff said, "Thanks for your help. There's a finders fee if you come up with something. Otherwise I'll have to pay you minimum two hundred dollars a day for your trouble."

They shook hands and Miguel left, while Jeff remained and finished his coffee.

While paying the check, Jeff said to himself, I'll nose around the docks myself. Maybe I'll get lucky.

He went to the docks, armed with Jeanne Golden's picture. He approached the fishermen working on their boats. They collected their catch and were separating them for sale. The air was permeated with the smell of fish. Sea gulls hovered overhead.

No one had any information. No one had picked anyone up at sea, just as Miguel had said.

"Es imposible, senior," the seasoned fishermen said. "It's too far. The water's too rough. Only the fish can survive."

Not giving up, Jeff went to the other side of the island. There were fewer fishermen there. The dock was old and in poor condition. Many boards had rotted away. The jetty was broken down, only a small piece remained. The water was very rough. Waves broke against the small fishing boats, causing them to roll from side to side, as they tried to reach land. The boats were vintage as was the fisherman's appearance. These old world men seemed to want to keep their way of life, no matter how hard.

Jeff asked the same questions. He added how sad this woman's family was. None of the men had any knowledge of a person being picked out of the water. As he started to leave, a short, gnarled, weather beaten man said quietly, "Amigo." Jeff approached him, picture in hand.

He hesitated and with deep sad dark eyes looked at Jeff and quietly said, "I don't want no trouble. No police! I tell you this for the family. Some months ago, while fishing, I picked up a lady from the water and put her in my boat. She was very sick. I brought her to the hospital and left her at the door."

He turned, walked away quickly, got into his fish filled truck, and drove away.

"Gracias, my amigo."

What a pity Jeff thought, to be so scared. This caring old guy brought her to the hospital, despite his fears. Lucky for me that the man had feelings.

-21-

Jeff arrived at the Central Hospital, the hospital closest to the dock. He approached the counter and asked for the medical director's office. He was ushered into Sr. Gonzalez's office. The reception area was paneled in light oak with several wooden chairs against the wall. The receptionist sat at an old fashioned intricately designed wooden desk, her computer on the table catty-cornered to the desk.

"Good morning miss." Using his most persuading antics, talking in a smooth low voice, looking into her eyes, giving her a broad smile, and out rightly flirting, he said, "My complements on your good taste of using such a beautiful desk. Most people used the new sleek standard ones."

She smiled and said, "May I help you."

"I have to see Dr. Gonzalez on a very important matter. Please do me this favor. You seem so caring and understanding."

He convinced her that this was a matter of utmost urgency, and she led him into the director's office. The charm worked.

"Thank you, senorita," he said as she left.

"Dr. Gonzalez, I am Jeff Atlas, private investigator for the Golden family from New York," he said, shaking hands. "I'm looking for a missing person believed to have been brought to your hospital. He gave him an envelope containing Jeanne's picture telling him what the fisherman had said about dropping the woman at the hospital entrance.

"Could I go about finding Jeanne through the hospital's records, sir?"

"I will speak to the staff and show them her picture, but unfortunately hospital records are out of the question. They are highly confidential. Don't worry. If someone has seen her she will be recognized."

"Thanks for your help," Jeff said. Not wanting to be a pest and annoy the doctor, he left the picture inside of the sealed envelope. He wrote the name of the hotel on the back of that envelope, which he gave to the director. "I look forward to hearing from you."

Dr. Gonzalez put the envelope on top of the pile of papers on his desk as he answered the ringing telephone.

Jeff left feeling optimistic. He called Sam with the good news. "Sam, Jeff here. I'm on a good lead, I think. Jeanne was brought to the Central Hospital..."

"Jeff, for real?" Sam yelled. The pounding of his heart made him feel as if it would burst.

"You bet. The Director assured me that he will show her picture to the staff for recognition. He is sure that if she was brought to this hospital, someone on staff would remember her. We'll be able to locate her soon."

"How, how...can I thank you?" Sam said his voice crackling with emotion, tears welling.

No problem—I'll keep in touch.

-22-

When Jeff got back to his hotel room, there was a message from Lina Gonzalez. He called the number on the tape.

"Sra. Gonzalez, this is Jeff Atlas."

"Sr. Atlas, I got your number from a friend, Mr. O'Hara in Aruba. He said you are a very thorough investigator and would be able to help me."

"What can I do for you?"

"I'm looking for information concerning a female called Marguerite. She was brought to Central Hospital as a fulana."

"A what?" he interrupted.

"Jane Doe, in Spanish. She has amnesia and can't remember her past. Is there a way that you can find any information about someone like her? I have nothing real to go on."

Jeff hesitated - his mind trying to process this coincidence. "Sra. Gonzalez, can we meet to talk about this? I'm at the Hilton."

"I'll meet you in the lounge in one hour."

Lina walked into the lounge and looked around. She was momentarily blinded going from the bright sunlight into the darkened area. Getting her bearings, she walked towards the large shiny bar. The room was nearly empty but for a man and woman seemingly in deep conversation, two women sipped their drinks and watched a movie on the television set, and a man concentrated on his beer at the bar.

"I'm looking for Jeff Atlas," she said to the bartender.

"I'm Atlas," Jeff said getting up from the stool.

"I'm Lina Gonzalez," she said shaking his hand.

"Can I buy you a drink Lina?" Jeff asked as he led her to a quiet table in the corner. A nice looking woman, he thought, tall, stately, self-assured.

"A margarita."

"A margarita and a beer," Jeff said to the bartender.

As they sipped their drinks, Jeff asked, "Why do you want to know about this missing lady?"

"Uh, it's personal."

"Nothing's personal if you want my help."

Taking a big gulp of her drink, Lina said, "Marguerite is seeing my brother. I think she's a gold digger. He's a big doctor and since he is alone she might be looking for an easy catch. I wonder if she may be hiding a sordid past."

"Have you met her?" Do you know what she looks like?" Jeff asked showing her Jeanne Golden's picture.

Lina felt as if she was hit in the face. Her mouth was agape. She stammered, "Where did you get her picture."

"I got it--"

She interrupted Jeff, "--her hair is short and gray, but it's her." She couldn't take her eyes' off of the picture.

"Let's calm down," he said. The color drained from her face. White as a sheet she suddenly appeared fragile.. "Catch your breath and listen to me. The lady in this picture is Jeanne Golden. She was in a boat crash last year in Aruba. Her husband has been looking for her. He hired me to try to find her. I just learned she was brought to Central Hospital."

Lina remained speechless. She couldn't believe this coincidence.

"Tell me about your brother," Jeff said needing some time to gather his thoughts.

"Ramon is a good man. He's the chief of internal medicine at the hospital, and respected in his field. He's never been married."

With a deep sigh, she told Jeff she needed another drink and started to relax as he went to the bar. When he returned with the drinks, she took a long sip of hers and continued still holding the glass in both hands. "He's a kind man and is good to all of us. He told us about this fulana; how she appeared at the hospital and almost died. He took a special interest in her, since she was all alone, and they became good friends."

"Do you know where she lives? I need to talk to her."

Lina hesitated, deep in thought, and said "I would like to talk to Ramon first. I don't want him to feel sorry for her. I would like to tell him she's married."

For the first time since she came into the bar she smiled.

-23-

"Molly, how nice to hear from you," Sam smiled when he heard her voice on the phone. "How've you been? I haven't gone to the last few meetings. Been preoccupied, but I do miss talking with you.

"Just great! Look, I have something to tell you. Would you meet me today?

"Sure, I need to talk to you too. I didn't eat breakfast yet. The coffee shop in an hour O.K.?"

"Thanks, Sam. I'll be there."

When Sam arrived Molly was already sitting in a booth, doodling on the paper place mat. *She looks lovely, attractive, not pretty but nice, so comforting* he thought. Slipping into the red naugahide booth, Sam echoed his thoughts, taking her hands in his. "You look great, Mol. A real sight for sore eyes as the saying goes." He suddenly realized how much he missed her.

"A decaf and cinnamon bagel with a schmeer, Mary," Sam ordered.

"The same for me," Molly said smiling.

As the waitress left, Sam blurted out, "I've been on a search for Jeanne."

Molly's expression changed. Her brown eyes took on a sad look and she played with the spoon in her hand.

"I hired a private investigator who's on to a good lead. Seems like he located an anonymous woman who was picked up at sea in Caracas, I'm so excited. He said the lead looks good."

Molly thought, *he's so into himself he doesn't even realize I called him to talk to me. He and Jeanne! My feelings really don't count.* Out loud, however, she said, "How nice for you. I hope your dream comes true."

On and on he rambled. "I might go to Caracas myself. I just can't sit here waiting for Atlas' call. I haven't even told Sara yet. Don't want to get her hopes up if it doesn't pan out. But I feel it will."

She politely waited, not wanting to interrupt. When Sam took a sip of coffee, she asked, "Atlas who?"

"The P.I. I hired, his name is Jeff Atlas. A real good guy!"

As he drank his coffee and bit into his bagel, Molly concentrated on hers.

"I'm leaving here," she said.

"Where are you running? Wait'll I finish my breakfast," he laughed with his mouth full of food.

"No Sam, I'm leaving New York. I'm moving to Florida. I decided I need a change. I'm going to my sister for awhile and will look for my own place."

"Florida," he said sputtering, the coffee dribbling down his chin. "So far? How come? I thought you loved New York. The museums, lectures, theater; our time together?"

"I do, but we really spend little time together. You have other friends." She paused hoping her meaning was clear. "And there are cultural things down south. Maybe not as good as here, but one can't have everything." Continuing as if rehearsed, she blandly said, "The children will visit me and I'll do the same. My sister will be close. I'll adjust. I'm good at it."

"When are you leaving?" he said, shaking his head putting the half eaten bagel back on the plate.

"At the end of the week. I'm packed and ready to go she said absently stirring her coffee, concentrating on the task.

Neither spoke for a few minutes, staring at each other. Sam held his coffee cup between both hands, looking straight into Molly's face. Her eyes filled. Her lips quivered as if she would start to cry. She suddenly rose from her chair, grabbed her coat, kissed Sam lightly on the lips and left the coffee shop.

He remained sitting as if paralyzed. *I didn't think I would miss her so much. It's as if she's already gone, he thought. I guess I took her for granted. It never dawned on me that she would go anywhere. I didn't realize how much she means to me. A real nice lady!* The waitress woke him from his thoughts when she brought the check. He paid the cashier and just left without his usual good-byes to Mary, his favorite waitress and a kibitz to Sal, the owner.

-24-

That evening he didn't go to the senior group meeting. He was troubled and his mind was filled with a myriad of thoughts; Jeanne, Molly, Jeff Atlas. The drone of the television sunk into the background. He barely heard it and certainly was not aware of the picture on the screen.

The insistent ringing of the doorbell finally got him off the chair.

Opening the door, he said, "Sylvia. What's wrong?" Looking at his watch, he exclaimed, "It's late."

"What's wrong with you? You weren't at the meeting. You didn't answer the phone. I was worried," she said walking directly into the hall.

"I'm O.K. Just didn't feel like going?"

"I'm here now, sweetie. I'll cheer you up," she said as she went into the living room sitting down on the gray velvet sofa. At least he's not with Molly. She wasn't at the meeting either, she thought. "Come sit by me. I missed you," she said patting the cushion.

Sam, feeling uncomfortable sat in an adjacent chair. "Sylvia..."

"Now, now -- bashful? Sitting so far away?"

When he didn't move, she said, "I'll make tea. Come show me where things are." Sylvia got up and kissed Sam on the forehead. She walked into the clean kitchen to fill the white flowered tea pot with water. She opened doors and drawers, took the necessary cups, plates and silverware and set the table. Sylvia spotted a box of Oreos and the tea bags and carried them to the table.

"Sam, where are you? Water's almost ready."

A weary Sam came into the kitchen. His brow wrinkled, his mouth set in a scowl and his hands by his sides, clenched into fists.

"Sylvia," he said in a loud controlled voice, "Please go home. I need to be alone. Please."

"Wh, wha, what's the matter?" she sputtered speechless for once, not believing that he was asking her to leave.

"My Jeanne may be alive," he blurted ashamed at his outburst.

"Nonsense," she said. She poured the hot water in each cup and composed herself by the time she put the teapot back on the burner. Sylvia watched the tea steep causing the water to turn a rusty brown and asked, "After all this time?"

"I hired a private investigator and he thinks he found her in Caracas."

"It's a hoax. He must be looking for money. How much are you paying him, and the doll? They'll take the money and she'll turn out to be someone else.

"Sylvia, how can you be so distrustful? You don't even know the man. How callous"

"I don't need to know him. He's a crook, that's what I know."

Completely depleted he said "Please go." She didn't believe what she heard and didn't move. He gently nudged her towards the front door. "I'll call you tomorrow."

"My goodness, *so emotional!*. O.K. I'll go but don't forget to call me." She tried to hug him but he backed away.

Once in bed, Sam found himself awake, staring at a print of Van Gogh's Blue Iris, which hung on a wall covered with yellow striped wallpaper. He tossed and turned, pulled the blanket, until he finally gave up and put the television on. A travelogue of South American cities was being shown. Caracas was the topic. "I'll be dammed," Sam said out loud. "Caracas." At that moment he felt something was pulling him to go there. I'll call the airlines in the morning he thought, and I'll go.

-25-

Lina went to see her brother Ramon. "Buenos Dias Maria," she said to his secretary.

"I'd like to see my brother."

"Si! Dr. Gonzalez, your sister is here," Maria said as she buzzed him on her intercom.

Opening his office door, he greeted Lina with a smile and a kiss on her cheek. "To what do I owe the pleasure of your company? You haven't been to visit me in a long time."

"I want to talk about Marguerite," she blurted out once they were in the privacy of his office. Not stopping to catch her breath she said, "I had a bad feeling about your friend and her mysterious past, so I met with a private investigator. He has information about a woman who vanished in a boating accident. He showed me a picture..."

"How dare you interfere in my life?" he screamed banging his fist on the desk. Jumping up he knocked the papers from his desk sending them sprawling onto the floor. He pointed his finger at her saying, "Sneak. You go to an investigator behind my back?" His voice cracked with anger. The veins in his neck extended.

Lina was startled. She had never seen her brother so angry. Her family usually kept their feelings in check.

"Leave," he yelled opening the door.

"But, but..."

"Go," he said pushing her out slamming the door.

He couldn't contain his emotions. He paced the office like an animal trapped in a cage.

Maria knocked gently, opening the door, as was her usual habit. "Are you all right?" she whispered, a surprised look on her face. He boss's face was beet red. His eyes looked wild. He paced in front of his desk. To herself she thought, *I have worked for him for ten years and have never heard such a row.* Out loud she calmly said, "Can I get you anything?"

Looking at her ashen face, he realized how he must have sounded and how wild he must look now; walking around the room with the papers strewn on the floor.

Taking a deep breath he said, "I'm O.K. Sorry for my outburst. I'm O.K., thanks."

She backed out of the office still looking at him.

As he picked up the mess, he came across the envelope the investigator left. Staring at the sealed envelope, afraid to open it, he tore it to shreds releasing his pent up emotions. I found the love of my life and I will not give it up, he screamed inside of himself.

-26-

Jeff Atlas appeared at Dr. Gonzalez' office the following morning, having given Lina time to talk to her brother. Maria buzzed, "Doctor, a private investigator is here to see you. He says it's a matter of utmost importance."

Hesitating for a moment he said, "Show him in Maria."

Dr. Gonzalez rose from his large brown leather chair and shook hands with Jeff. He was ashamed to tell that he tore the picture and instead said, "I've been so busy I forgot to look at the picture, and now it seems as if I misplaced the envelope. We're short two staff doctors and I've been filling in for them. Sorry," he said sheepishly.

"Not to worry." Showing the picture to the doctor, Jeff said "I have solid reason to believe this lady was brought to your hospital many months ago with no memory of past events."

Dr. Gonzalez shook as he saw the picture of Jeanne Golden. "Mi Marguerite," he barely whispered, remaining fixed in one place. "I never associated the two when you were last here," he said, even though in his heart of hearts he knew. His sister had planted the thought. Still staring at the picture, he said, "You say that her husband is looking for her? *Mi amor is married?*" A sob escaped as he tried not to cry. His mouth remained open as he concentrated on the picture he held in a tremulous hand.

"I'm sorry Doc," Jeff said. "I didn't mean to startle you."

Ramon flopped back into the chair leaning his head against the back as if in defeat. His eyes clouded over and the Picasso sketch on the far wall was blurred. He squirmed in the chair and finally leaned on the desk, holding his head in his hands. He muttered "What will I do now?"

Jeff said, "Does she know who she is?"

Dr. Gonzalez shook his head no.

"Do you think it's for real or is she playing a game?"

"Playing a game? How dare you insult her," he said sitting straight up, in a voice filled with anguish.

"I'd like to meet her," Jeff said. It might be easier for me, as a stranger, to talk with her."

"Never" Ramon said in a loud agitated tone, slamming his fist down on the desk.

The ferocity of his voice startled Jeff, whose body gave a little jump from the comfortable chair. "O.K., O.K. Don't get excited." He removed a metal flask from his attaché case and filled two small paper cups with vodka. "Here Doc. It'll calm your nerves," he said handing a cup to Ramon. "I always keep a little something for an emergency."

With one gulp the cup was empty. Jeff's too. They were both quiet for a few minutes calming from the effect of the liquor. Jeff stood looking out of the window at the Boulevard with the hordes of people hurrying and scurrying about. The blasting of a siren from a fire truck broke the silence. Turning back towards the desk, Jeff said kindly, "Take the picture and go talk to your friend. Call me later."

"Gracias," Ramon said lapsing into his familiar language.

He remained motionless, as Jeff left the office. Dr. Gonzalez focused on the picture, which reflected a pretty woman with blonde hair and a big smile wrinkling her face in a pleasant way. She appeared very happy. He thought, *she looked happy then and now my Marguerite is finally starting to look happy. Now this shock. How will she take it? A husband? A husband! I didn't even ask about this man. Is he a good man? Did she purposely leave him? A year! I love this woman. What now?* His head was aching with the mass of jumbled thoughts roaming his mind.

He removed Marguerite's picture from his wallet. They had taken pictures of each other at the carnival a few months' ago. He held them next to each other trying to find a reason for them not being the same women.

After many minutes, which felt more like hours, he picked up the telephone and called her.

-27-

"Good morning. Would you like a pillow?" the stewardess said to Sam.

"No thank you. I'm quite comfortable. This aisle seat gives me room for my feet."

The plane was air bound and the usual airplane banter accompanied the distribution of blankets, pillows, newspapers, headsets, and safety announcements. "Thank goodness it's finally quiet," Sam said to the man in the middle seat. "I'm Sam Golden."

"Michael Thompson," the man mumbled, without even turning his head, burrowing himself deeper into his newspaper.

Sam got the message and closed his eyes. *Soon I'll see her -- I feel it.* He was very excited to be on his way to Venezuela. He had left a dispatch for Jeff Atlas with his arrival plans.

Another blaring announcement broke into his thoughts. "There's a problem with our scheduled film. In its place we will feature the classic *Sabrina.* Sorry for any inconvenience."

Audrey Hepburn's, William Holden's, and Humphrey Bogart's faces on the screen brought a sharp memory of his wife. Hepburn and Bogart were her favorite actors and this was her special movie. She had seen it dozens of times. Jeanne loved the ending when Bogart leaves the boardroom in search of Sabrina. Their kiss always brought a tear to Jeanne's eyes. *Of all the current pictures to show this one is playing. What a coincidence.*

The thoughts brought new fears. His mind worked overtime. He sat staring straight ahead with his eyes open not seeing anything. *If its Jeanne, will she be the same? It's been more than a year since she's gone. I can no longer hear her voice or see her face clearly. I lost her smile. After the accident, in my mind, I was able to feel her kiss. No longer! Will she know me? Will I be a stranger to her? Will she love me? Do I still love her? Will it show? I've been with other women. Are my feelings real or just a memory?*

Sam removed the picture of Jeanne that he took in Aruba from his wallet and stared at it trying to recapture the live Jeanne. Giving an unconscious shudder, he remembered the reason for Aruba. *Her affair and mine-- so long ago! Would we have resolved the past had the accident not occurred?*

The feeling of a presence nearby and the smell of coffee brought Sam back to the present. "Excuse me sir," the stewardess tapped his shoulder. "Would you care for a drink?"

Still stuck in his ruminations, he hesitated. "Uh, a Bloody Mary!"

The liquor calmed him and he closed his eyes, listening through the earphones to the dialogue of the movie. Molly's face broke into his intimate thoughts. *I can see her more clearly than I can see Jeanne.* He remembered the coffee *with Molly and wished she was here to comfort him. She has such a positive attitude. He now felt all alone. I'd even be glad to see Sylvia at this moment.* "Her drivel cheers me up," he chuckled out loud.

"Excuse me," the woman seated across the aisle said, removing her earphones.

"I'm sorry to have disturbed you. I'm Sam Golden."

"I'm Mary Smith. That's my real name," she said, laughing. "Not a made up moniker. When I introduce myself, sometimes people think I use a pseudonym."

He smiled. "I'm going to Caracas. How about you?"

"Same place," she said. "I'm meeting friends. We'll vacation on the beach for two weeks. I'm so looking forward to it..."

"Take your seats. Fasten your seatbelts. Prepare for landing." This announcement abruptly ended their conversation.

He tried to see the land below, but his seat was too far away from the window. His doubts increased as the plane flew over the Caracas airspace. *I'll have to wait to see what will happen, he thought with a sigh. I'm suddenly afraid to face the unknown.*

-28-

A taxi took Sam to the hotel. His room was sumptuously decorated. The pale bronze carpet, plush beneath his feet, was the same shade as the bedcovering. The monotone colors put him momentarily at ease. He left a message for Jeff, and called room service. While unpacking he had a strange longing for human connection, *"sort of like a port in a storm,"* he thought. The idea of a storm and that fateful day left him drained of all energy. Sam desperately needed company but didn't know who to call. Molly again broke into his thoughts and he sat down at the desk to write to her. He addressed the letter to her old address. I guess her mail will be forwarded, he thought.

Dear Molly,

I've just arrived in Venezuela. It's probably as hot here as it's going to be in Florida. Mol, I'm here to see a woman who they think is Jeanne. I'm scared to see this lady. I've got all kinds of doubts. I wish you were here to reassure me; you're so good at it. I miss you. The plane ride was long and tedious, filled with different thoughts. I'm so mixed up.

Suddenly Sam felt he was rambling, not knowing what he really wanted to write or whether he even wanted to. He tore it and tossed it. *Why is Molly so much a part of me now? We were never even intimate. I thought of her as a good friend. Did I make a mistake? And what about Jeanne?*

Frustrated he paced until his food arrived; the old standby burger and fries with strong Spanish coffee. He finished his dinner, and having nothing else to do, got into the comfortable bed, heaved a sigh, and turned the television on. He didn't realize the programs would be in Spanish which he couldn't understand. Can't win here either crossed his mind. He clicked the power off and opened his book, Hemingway's; *For Whom The Bells Toll.* A Hemingway aficionado, re-reading the books somewhat comforted him. In a few minutes he was asleep with his glasses on his nose and the open book leaning on his face.

-29-

The same evening, Ramon Gonzalez and Marguerite Perez were at dinner. She needed a surname in order to file immigration papers. Perez sounded good to her. They drank several glasses of red wine with dinner and were feeling mellow. The soft overhead lights and the flicker of the votive candle on the gold muted paisley cloth created a relaxed atmosphere.

"Dearest, I have something serious to discuss with you," Ramon said while waiting for their coffee.

She smiled, hoping it would be a proposal. The scenes of their recent intimacy crept though her thoughts. He excited her with his lovemaking and made her feel secure with his softness and tenderness. She now knew she was in love and felt ready even without a past.

He didn't know how to begin. He took her hands in his, looked into her eyes, and said slowly and quietly, "I know who you are."

The silence was deafening. Marguerite was numb and didn't move except for her change of expression. The smile disappeared. The color drained from her face. She pulled her hands away knocking over the wine glass. A river of red liquid ran over the gold cloth. Neither moved to stop it! She jumped as the wine slid from the cloth to her knees, but remained immobile still in shock.

Ramon grabbed his napkin and tried to sop it up.

"Stop," she yelled pushing him away. "How? When?" she said in a shaky voice. Without waiting for an answer, she said "Who am I?"

He hesitated then said, "Jeanne Golden. You're an American from New York City." Ramon didn't have the strength to continue.

"And?" she asked emphatically.

"There is a Mr. Golden," he said suddenly sitting straight up, his voice getting stronger. He needed to give her the details without letting his feelings interfere.

"Sam is his name. He hired an investigator to find you -- it seems there was a boat accident and you were lost. A fisherman pulled you to safety and left you at the hospital. The rest you know." He took out the picture and showed it to her. "Here is a picture of you as Jeanne Golden."

Marguerite's hand shook as she stared at the image on the paper. She threw the picture down on the table as if it burned her. She looked directly into Ramon's eyes as hers overflowed with tears. He had no words of comfort. He needed comforting himself.

The waiter broke the mood by putting their coffee cups in front of them. "Would you care for any dessert?" he asked.

"No... just the check!" Ramon answered quickly still looking at Marguerite.

The moment passed. "What else do you know?" she whispered with a parched throat.

"Nothing! But I'll take you to meet Mr. Atlas, the investigator, and see what he knows. For now let's go home."

She clung to him as they left the restaurant. Getting into the car she wouldn't let go. He had to pry her hands off of him to get her into the seat.

Ramon took a scared, shaken Marguerite to her house. The apartment was sparsely furnished with mismatched pieces, although clean and organized. The kitchen opened to the left and a small bedroom on the right. They sat on a tan simulated leather couch adorned with red, gold, and black pillows; the outcome of Marguerite's efforts to brighten up the dingy apartment with a minimum of money. The small coffee table held a vase with plastic flowers and a gold covered candy dish filled with chocolates which were her passion. The floor was bare except for a cotton multi-colored area rug in the middle.

"What kind of a life did I lead?" she questioned.

"Try not to obsess on it. We'll find out soon enough."

"Don't treat me like a child," she snapped back, raising her voice. "Wouldn't you worry? Why can't I remember?" she said, banging her head in frustration. "Did I do something so terrible I had to dismiss it from my mind?"

"Mi amor, let me make us cafe con leche, your favorite," Ramon asked not knowing how to help her. "We'll talk about your fears."

As he prepared the coffee, he thought about his own fears. *What if she remembers her husband and wants to go with him? What if she really did something terrible? It's not fair for me to impose my feelings now and further confuse her. It might influence her decision.*

"Ramon, I need you. I'm shaking all over."

He brought in the coffee and sat beside her, their shoulders touching.

"The coffee is delicious," she said breathing out a deep sigh. She held the cup in both hands, taking comfort from the warmth. Thank you," she said sheepishly.

"De nada."

*

Looking straight into his deep black eyes, she kissed him softly on the lips. He responded and their bodies intertwined. Instinctively they went together into the bedroom, dropping their clothes as they walked, and made passionate love. They explored each other. He found ways to bring out the wildness she so expertly hid. They reached new crescendos that they had never achieved before. Their bodies melted into each other, forming one person.

When their release came, they lay exhausted in each others' arms, her head resting comfortably on his chest. Her fingers gently toyed with his graying chest hairs.

"Don't leave me," she whispered in a husky voice. "Stay here. I love you like I have loved no other."

Ramon breathed evenly as sleep took over. She wondered if he had heard her.

During the night they awoke and made love again, this time more tenderly; less rushed, less intense.

In the morning, while Marguerite prepared for dressing, Ramon called Jeff Atlas to make an appointment. "Marguerite, we have to be in the investigator's office at eleven," Ramon yelled, over the running of the shower.

-30-

Jeff called Sam in the early morning. "Sam, can you be here at eleven? I'll fill you in on all that's happened."

"Sure. Where are you?" I'm sharing the office with Miguel Corrado. You remember he's the P.I. I have been in contact with here in Venezuela. It's 34 Olivaro Street, next to the Cinema, third floor. It's not too far from the hotel." He didn't mention that Jeanne Golden would be there as well.

Jeff pondered as he picked up his coffee and buttered roll from the cart outside of the building. *Since neither Sam nor Jeanne knows the other will be here at the same time, their reactions should be spontaneous. I hope my plan won't backfire.*

Promptly at eleven, Sam knocked on the door. He was neatly dressed with khaki casual pants and a white short sleeved shirt. The two men shook hands, and Jeff could feel the tension in Sam's handshake.

"Did you have a hard time finding the office?" Jeff asked. He hoped that the mundane conversation would put Sam at ease.

As Sam looked around, he took in the smartly furnished office, with the usual brown leather chair and functional wooden desk holding the ever present computer. "The cab driver found it with no trouble."

"Can I get you some coffee?" he asked stalling for time.

"I'm fine. Tell me what's going on."

Jeff settled in the large chair, picked up a pen and played with it as he said, "I spoke to someone who knows this woman. He assures me that he will speak with her and..."

The knock on the door caught their attention. Both men turned in time to see Marguerite and Ramon enter the office.

"Come in, come in," Jeff said standing up.

Marguerite was dressed in the Spanish style. Her multi-colored print flared skirt was accompanied by a white blouse that just grazed her shoulders. Her hair, recently dyed a pleasant colored light blonde, was pulled back from her face. Some tendrils escaped breaking the severe look. Her blue eyes shined, with her recently discovered happiness, despite her fears of the unknown.

Sam remained in the twisted position, eyes fixed as if seeing a ghost. He gasped and held his heart. He tried to stand but could not. He had turned to stone. His rubbery legs would not hold his weight.

"Jeanne?" he whispered, holding onto the arms of the chair to give him support, barely having the breath to get the word out.

Jeff ran to get Sam water, afraid he would faint.

Ramon held Marguerite tightly. There was no sign of recognition in her demeanor, except for a slight twitch in her left eye.

She felt a tightness in her chest and remained standing, expressionless, staring at Sam's pallid face.

Ramon, surprised at her lack of emotion, assumed she was in shock.

"Please sit," Jeff said wiping his forehead with a handkerchief. He didn't know how to start the conversation. Jeff who was never at a loss of words, was overcome by the look on Sam's face. "Sam, are you all right?"

There was no response. Sam couldn't take his eyes off Jeanne. After a long silence, he asked her accusingly. "Where have you been?" "I'm out of my mind looking for you. I've looked all over. I thought you were dead," he cried, tears washing down his face.

"I'm sorry," she said, "I don't know you." She looked at Ramon, as if to elicit some help. He squeezed her hand in support.

"Don't know me!" Sam yelled finally getting up from the chair. "We've been married for forty years with a daughter and two grandchildren. We've had a life together, and you can only say, I don't know you!" He sat down in a defeated motion, holding his head in his hands.

"I'm sorry," she said, turning away, her voice devoid of feeling. "I can't remember,"

Jeff didn't know how to react. "Doc, can you help out here?"

While wrestling with his own emotions, Ramon said, "Mr. Golden, I'm very sorry that things have not turned out as you would have liked."

Sam remained motionless, still in shock over the scene that just took place.

Marguerite got up to leave. She appeared shaken, cold. "I have to go," she said. "I need to get out of here."

Ramon stood and took her arm as they headed for the door.

Sam asked in a surprisingly loud voice, "You will come back. You won't disappear again."

"I assure you we'll be back," Ramon said sympathetically.

They left Sam still sitting in the same position, pain and confusion showing in his face. Jeff thought that his new friend aged ten years in the last ten minutes.

"I don't understand it," Sam mumbled over and over, nodding his head.

*

Jeff left Sam at his hotel and sat in his car pondering the morning's occurrences; listening to the strains of "Mona Lisa" on the radio. Jeff had found a station that played music from his era. Even though the words were sung in Spanish, the music was his forte, a throwback from the '50's. He needed time to understand the significance of the encounter. As he put the past few hours in order, Sam's emotional reaction was certainly understandable. His feelings were written all over his face. The way he paled when he saw her. The loss of words, the inability to move, the almost hysterical outburst. But her! Jeanne or Marguerite was definitely cold as ice, empty of all emotion, except for an instant flicker of an eye. What did that mean? Maybe nothing!

But on the other hand I don't know her. Is this her natural manner or is she really confused as to who this man is? After all, here was someone who was a complete stranger, so she said, claiming to be her husband and father of her child. "What the hell, maybe that's it," he said aloud starting the car. Pulling out of the parking spot he thought, *I hope I'll be able to understand more at the next meeting.*

-31-

Ramon took Marguerite for a ride out of the city in an attempt to calm her. Although her appearance seemed calm, her hands shook and her voice sounded a little hysterical. They rode out to the beach and stopped at a restaurant on the pier. They sat in a corner table near the window. The wood plank tables had silverware wrapped in white paper napkins. It had the look of a real beach shack.

"Marguerite, are you O.K.?"

"Sure," she answered sarcastically staring out of the window. "This man says he's my husband. How do I know that? A stranger to me... a child? Is it possible? I would know that I had a child, wouldn't I?" She seemed to be completely confused.

They sipped their margaritas in silence and picked on a lunch of seafood paella. The steady rhythm of the water hitting the rocks comforted her. Being a weekday, the restaurant and beach were almost deserted, except for some women with young children wading and playing with pails and shovels.

Looking out at the water, Marguerite said, "Could I have survived out there? Am I such a good swimmer?" She shook her head in disbelief, her whole body quivered.

"Miracles do happen, querida," Ramon said between bites of the spicy fish. "There have been occasions where people were rescued from the water." *What a mundane statement,* he thought. His inept attempt to cheer her up fell as flat as the tortillas in the basket.

"After lunch, let's walk on the beach," Ramon said, getting a second wind. He forced himself to be cheerful though his whole future might someday blow up in his face. "The sun is bright and maybe we'll be able to relax."

"Whatever."

Strolling along the beach, with a soft breeze blowing at their faces, she suddenly stopped, "Can they force me to go with him, a total stranger? And if I have a child, shouldn't I want to see her? Help me, help me," she cried raising her arms to the sky as if looking to heaven for some sign.

Feeling helpless, Ramon said nothing. After a few moments he finally said, "I think we need a lawyer."

She ignored his suggestion. "You're the doctor. Will it ever come back? Am I doomed to a life of now and no before?"

He shrugged his shoulders. "I have done some research on amnesiacs. Hypnosis is a possibility, although not always successful. It works well with some, but a few never regain their memory, no matter what the treatment. I didn't say anything before because to tell the truth, I'm afraid of the past and what it could do to us..."

"Maybe I did something awful," Jeanne blurted in horror.

Ramon tried to comfort her with a story. "My past has been anything but perfect. Let me tell you..."

Not really in the mood to hear his tale of woe, she acquiesced and surrendered herself to the colorful blanket Ramon bought from a peasant on the beach.

"Many years ago, in South America, while still in my twenties doing my residency, I became acquainted with a woman. She was beautiful with magnificent brown eyes that looked right into my soul. I was immediately hooked--"

Marguerite broke in annoyed. "Do I have to hear about your love affairs right now?"

"You have to listen," he said patronizing her. "We dated seriously for a few months," he continued, changing his position to avoid the sun. "I didn't have much time away from the hospital and was usually tired when I did. But, we managed. We laughed, took walks, danced the night away and when we could made wild passionate love at every opportunity. She soon moved into my apartment. I felt I knew everything I needed to know about her. There never seemed to be time..."

"Ramon, I'm dying of thirst. That paella was spicy. Would you get me a soda from that man?" Marguerite said, pushing her sweaty hair from her face.

Annoyed at the interruption, he got up, kicked some sand, and bought two Cokes. Seeing his displeasure, she said meekly. "Sorry. I seem to be saying that a lot lately. It'll get better," Under her breath, she mumbled, "I hope."

Still bent on telling her of his prior experience, he continued where he left off. "Looking back I realize that she did ask me about my life; where I lived, how I lived, what my family did. Things like that. I told her many personal things, which I now know I shouldn't have. I bragged how my family had some money and I didn't have to work while I went to med school.

Taking a deep breath, he took Marguerite's hands in his and said, "I swore never to talk again about personal stuff, but seeing how I feel about you, I must."

"Ramon, I don't want that responsibility. I have enough on my plate."

"Sorry, my turn now," he said wiping the perspiration from his face and taking his jacket off. His tie, which he had removed before, hung out of the breast pocket. The sharp edge of his voice and the wild look in his eyes made her wince and pay attention.

"One day I came home early in the evening, which was unusual. My days as a resident blended into nights and then it was morning again and I was still at the hospital. But this evening I got a reprieve. I entered my apartment and found male apparel strewn over the living room floor. I followed its trail to the bedroom where I found my love in the act of sexual fulfillment. Appalled and in shock, I flung the first thing I could lay my hands on. Unfortunately it was the lamp which was the only source of light in the room except for a sliver from the living room. "Get out," I yelled. "Get out. He jumped naked out of the bed, trying to grab his underwear in the dark. She remained sitting awkwardly pulling the blanket to cover her. What a sight." He chuckled at the memory, but Marguerite saw the hurt in his eyes. "She remained sitting with the blanket covering her."

"I ran out into the street not knowing where to go. I ran until I was too exhausted to move. Stopping to catch my breath, I found myself in front of a bar. I went in and got stinking drunk and to top things off, I was mugged."

"Poor baby," Marguerite said, patting his face. "How awful -- what she did to you. What did you do with no money?"

"After I puked my guts out, I called my brother, Juan. He took me to his house and I slept like a baby. I missed my shift at the hospital and had to face a reprimand from the senior resident." Ramon filled with anger during the retelling of the experience and reliving his humiliation, spit saliva with each sentence.

Trying to calm him down, Marguerite said with a shiver, "I'm getting cold," a sudden dark cloud passed over. "Let's go."

*

As they approached her apartment, they noticed a note stuck in the door.

Looking at each other, she read it aloud. "Can we meet alone? I have to speak to you. The Hilton, Room 514. Sam."

"Should I go?"

"You have to face him sometime. Maybe this would be as good a time as any."

"But I can't go now," she said procrastinating. "I have to hear the end of your story. You were so determined to tell it, there must be some point you want me to hear."

Needing something to do, Marguerite made coffee. She was hooked on the strong hot liquid. While waiting for the brew, she set the table with two white mugs and cake plates. "Talk to me," she said, filling their cups. "I want to hear about what's her name," she laughed trying to make light of it. "You never told me her name, by the way."

"Not important," he said. "When I returned the next day," he continued obsessed as if he had never stopped talking, "she was gone. There was a note on the kitchen table that said, "you told me your family has money, I need some. Send $10,000 to a post office box." The letter threatened in the event I didn't want to pay, the police would be interested to know that she was only sixteen years old.

"Oh no," Marguerite gasped. "Statutory rape!"

"You can imagine how ridiculous I felt sharing my bed with a teenager. I was appalled. How could I have been so fooled? I didn't know where to find her. I didn't even know whether it was her real name. I panicked and thought my career was over before it began."

Marguerite washed the dishes as he spoke, trying to hide the shock on her face.

"Not knowing where to turn, I told my brothers. We came up with a plan for them to watch the mailbox and to scare her. We reasoned that paying her would be a life long punishment, which I could ill afford. Nor did I deserve it. I was only a little more than a kid myself and certainly not worldly. This was my first experience.'

"To make a long story short, they confronted her and did pay her $1000 which was a lot of money in those days. But she had to sign a statement that there was no physical contact between us."

"How did they stop her? Did they hurt her?"

"They grabbed her in the post office, took her for a ride and told her they had connections, mentioning the name of a reputed gangster. They really didn't know him- just used it to scare her. Juan and Cesar told her if she wanted to live, she should leave the area, and not return. I never heard from her again."

She smiled, "Remind me never to tangle with your brothers." Hugging him, she said, "I'm glad things worked out well for you and me, not the mystery woman."

"Now you know why I've been so cool. I was so hurt. I've been afraid to trust again. I've lived so many years alone. I was just beginning to let my guard down and now..."

"Shut up," she said, kissing him. "I'll meet this man, Sam and explain to him that I don't know him and that will be that."

-32-

Sam sat slumped on the beige striped wing chair in the darkened hotel room. He had gone to see Jeanne to try to assure her who he was. When she wasn't home, on an impulse he left her a note to meet him. *Maybe if she and I were alone, with no outside interferences, she would remember.*

The shrill ring of the telephone startled him, and he jumped from the chair. He could not find the phone for a few seconds. It had rung only once before in this strange room, and since he was confused and still engrossed in his plan to meet Jeanne, he didn't know where it was. Sam had turned into an old man in the flick of an eye. Shuffling toward the noise, he picked up the phone.

"Dad, Dad its Sara. Are you all right? What are you doing in Caracas? We just got home from Disney and I found your message," she said, all in one breath.

"You're with a friend. What friend?"

"Saraleh, shhh. I'm fine, fine. Let me get a word in edgewise."

"Daddy, I'm so worried about you. I just spoke to you a few days ago from vacation, and you never said a word..."

"Sara, you always talk too fast. Give me a chance."

Taking a deep breath, she said "Sure, sure go ahead."

"I've been having this feeling in the back of my head that your mother is still alive somewhere..."

"Alive?" Sara yelled so loud that Sam almost dropped the phone. "My mother!" The voice turned into a shriek and Sam started to cry.

"Please sweetheart --. I didn't want to scare you. Don't cry, my precious -- let me finish." Sam controlled his fright and continued in a forced loud voice, although in a soft tone. "I hired an investigator who said there was a woman in this city who just appeared with no memory of her past. She fit Mom's description, so here I am."

After a long silence-- "So Daddy, what happened?" Sara said in a voice so slow it didn't seem like her.

"I haven't met her yet," he lied. I can't hurt her and tell her that her mother doesn't remember her, he thought. "It'll take a few more days. She's not here right now, but I'm making arrangements. I'm sorry to have scared you. You've been hurt by all of this. It pains me to see my baby so unhappy. You're still my baby, you know," he said with feigned levity.

"Daddy, what can I say? Wait. I'll come to you and we can see this woman together. I'll make arrangements for the children and I'll..."

"No." Sam's tone was emphatic. Realizing how he must sound, he softened. "I, I mean," he stammered, "It's too soon. It probably isn't her. I'm an old man living in a dream world. I'll see this mystery woman and I'll call you, I promise. Stay with my darling grandchildren. They need you. Don't waste your time on what will likely be a false lead."

"But I want to be with you. You shouldn't be alone, or are you really with a friend?"

"No. I just said that to throw you off the track. But I'm O.K. Honey, believe me. Look, I'll come to visit you as soon as this is over. The lead is likely to fizzle. I just needed to try one more time. This call is costing you a fortune. I'll say good-bye and promise to call you tomorrow, although it doesn't seem likely that I'll see her yet. Kiss the kids-- I'll call you -- I promise. I love you. Don't worry."

Sam hung the phone up before she could answer. *I've told her such a lie, I feel awful. But how could I hurt her again? Better she shouldn't know yet, he thought. Maybe better I shouldn't know.*

O.K. What do I do now? Sit by the telephone waiting for Jeanne to call me? Will she call me?

Sitting back down in the comfortable wing chair, he picked up USA Today, and looked at the paper without concentrating on one word. He called room service for a bottle of Scotch and a bucket of ice. Within minutes, it arrived, and he immediately poured himself two drinks. He could feel his whole body relax, the stiffness became soft; the tension left his face. Heaving a deep sigh, his shoulders dropped into their natural position, his jaw slackened, the worry lines around his eyes disappeared and he lost that old man demeanor.

Not being a man who usually drank liquor, the effect was immediate. After the third drink, the empty glass slipped from his hand, dropping onto the soft carpet. He settled into a deep sleep, his head resting on his heaving chest. A loud snore of an inebriated man occasionally escaped.

-33-

The next morning Sam showered, shaved and was dressing when he heard a tap. He opened the door to find himself face to face with Jeanne.

"Good morning." Seeing his open shirt, she asked, "I hope I didn't catch you at a bad time."

"No, no. Come in." He fastened the last button on his shirt. Sam inhaled her fragrance as she walked in, a soft flowery bouquet almost like roses. His pulse raced. *It's not her usual scent he thought, but then it's been a long time.*

"Can I get you a drink? The mini bar has soda, water..."

"Nothing thanks. You wanted to meet me alone?"

"We need to talk without the interference of outside parties. Perhaps you will remember me if I can tell you about us," he said in the strained voice of a desperate man. "Please sit."

Not knowing how to proceed, Sam took a Coke and played with removing the cap, trying to get his thoughts together. He slowly sipped the cool liquid and sat down to face her.

As she waited for him to start to talk, she looked around the room taking in the subtle shades of beiges, the monotone made her feel cold and sad. There was nothing personal about this space. Sitting on the edge of the chair, she blurted, "I need to know about my daughter, if I am who you say I am. What is she like? How old is she? Is she tall, short, thin, fat, blonde? Things like that." Relieved at breaking the silence, she squirmed in the chair trying to relax, while her insides were on fire.

"She's a wonderful girl. Her name is Sara, after your mother. She's thirty-eight, married to a very nice man, Bob McKenna. They live in Burlington, Massachusetts, and have two beautiful children, Brianna and Jeremy. They're ten and twelve." He stopped to take a breath as he thought how indifferent this description sounds, like talking to a stranger. *But yet she is like a stranger.* He shook his head as if to get rid of the cobwebs in his brain and continued. "You would love them."

"What kind of mother can I be, if I don't know my own child?"

86

Jeanne whimpered absently shredding the tissue she held.

"Don't be silly, you're a marvelous mother, honey," Sam said, slipping back into using the familiar expression.

She blanched at the endearment.

"Only you're ill now," he continued. "When you get better you'll remember. You have too. I need you."

A knock on the door caused them to turn towards the entry hall. He got up and opened the door.

"Ramon, uh Dr. Gonzalez" Sam said, with his mouth agape showing his surprise. Holding the door ajar, he said in a voice tinged with icicles, "What can I do for you?"

"Marguerite came here alone. I want to make sure she's OK," Ramon said, in the same icy tone as he tried to peer into the room.

"What do you think I would do to her?" Sam asked, raising his voice.

"Can I come in?" Ramon pushed Sam out of the way walking into the suite.

"Ramon," Jeanne said standing up. "I told you I need to be alone with Sam. I have to hear things only he can tell me."

"I don't know if it's safe here, knowing his frame of mind and how desperate he is to have you."

"Wait a minute," Sam yelled, his body tensing, hands clenched into fists, "Who the hell do you think you are bursting in here and accusing me."

As he walked towards Ramon, she could see Sam's body language change. His face turned beet red -- eyes luminous -- staring at his opponent -- hands raised as if ready to pounce.

Ramon sensing the coming attack turned and faced Sam as if he was preparing for a clash. He took a few steps and came face to face with Sam. The two men challenged each other without words, fists on the ready. Their bodies took the position of fighters, shoulders hunched, feet firm, as they confronted each other.

"Please, please," Jeanne said taking a few steps getting between them. "Have some feeling for me. I can't stand it if you fight," her voice raising into a hysterical pitch. Glaring at them she spewed, "You both stay here acting like little boys. I'm leaving." She grabbed her purse and ran out.

*

Getting off of the elevator in the hotel lobby, she looked for the ladies' room. Washing her face with cold water calmed her. She found solace in this empty impersonal space. Sitting on the settee covered in a mauve print, she leaned her head back and closed her eyes. The rhythmical throbbing of her pulse started to taper off, and she felt her whole body slack. Her mind, however, operated in double speed.

Hearing the door open, she opened her eyes to see a woman entering. Looking around, she spied a bank of telephones and automatically got up as if in a trance.

She sat on a stool in front of a phone for some time, picking up the receiver and putting it down, not able to decide what to do. Finally with a determined air, she dialed information, "Robert McKenna, Burlington, Massachusetts, United States." With trepidation and shaking fingers, she dialed the number. "Hello," a soft female voice answered. "Hello, who's there?" She was unable to answer and hung up the phone quietly.

-34-

Marguerite took the bus home rather than a taxi. She needed time to ponder her future. Deep in thought, she wasn't aware of her surroundings. Since it was lunch hour, the bus was filled with people. All of the seats were taken and many people stood hovering over the seated throng. The steady movement lulled her into a relaxed state. As her body slowed, she felt the dripping perspiration on her face, causing mascara to blur her vision. She ignored it and closed her eyes.

How could I not recognize my daughter's voice? I hoped if I heard her talk it would come back to me. Now what do I do? Her thoughts jumped from one to another. *Do I go to be with my child? Do I go back to Sam? Do I stay with Ramon, my love? What good would I be to a family I don't know? But - is it fair for them to know me and me not them? How would I fit in?*

She mused each alternative and concentrated so hard that she missed her stop and had to walk back to her apartment. As she put the key in the lock, she gasped and sprung away in surprise at hearing a man's voice. Ramon yelled, in a sharp voice, "Where were you?"

Marguerite seized her chest, and in a high piercing voice screamed, "What are you doing here?"

"You scared me half to death," he said coming towards her.

"I took the bus..."

"Don't ever go away again without telling me."

She was a pack of nerves from the news she had to digest and the decisions she had to make. This intrusion and accusation caused her to react in a way he had never seen before.

"Now, just a minute! Who do you think you are? My boss! I don't have to report to you," her face reddened as she spat out the words. "Don't give me orders."

He tried to take her in his arms, but she shrugged him away. "This can do no good." She walked into the kitchen, filled the coffee pot with water and banged the can on the counter in a defiant motion. "Give me space," Jeanne yelled.

"I didn't mean anything. You frightened me. It's so not like you to run away." He raised his hands in a helpless gesture.

The mundane task of making coffee calmed her. She felt she had overreacted, looked at Ramon and said, "What happened between you guys?"

"Nothing," he responded with a slow smile. "When you chastised us, the mood changed. We realized at our age how silly we looked, neither of us being a fighter. The thought of what might have happened if one of us got in a lucky punch and actually hit each other made me laugh. The laugh broke the tension. We parted amicably, but we'll never be friends. Too much competition!"

"Ramon, after much soul searching and today's events, I made up my mind to start hypnosis. I owe it to my daughter to try all avenues, so that I might remember her," Marguerite said, fussing with the dishes.

"Are you sure about that?" Once you start you might not like what you encounter."

"I'm willing to take a chance. I have to gamble that the news will be good. I have too much to lose."

"Leave it to me. I know a therapist and I'll make the appointment, Ramon said, kissing her gently on the cheek. "Let's drink the coffee. The aroma is calling me."

-35-

Sam answered the phone on the third ring, to hear his daughter's voice.

"Hi Dad."

"Sara is everything all right?"

"Fine here -- and by you? I haven't heard from you and I've been on pins and needles waiting to see if the woman is Mom."

With a deep breath, he made a quick decision and answered, "No. She resembles her but is a stranger to me."

"I'm disappointed," she said in a cracking voice. "At first I thought you were crazy to pursue this lead. But as time went on, I started to dream. In the back of my mind I almost believed, but now..."

"Sara, I'm sorry."

There was a long pause and deliberately changing the subject, Sara said, "Are you coming home? I need to see you. You're all I have."

"Nonsense! Don't be silly. You have your family."

In a little girl's shrill voice, she said, "You'll always be my Daddy, with a special place in my heart."

With tears starting to smart, Sam said, "Honey..." He stopped short, remembering the confrontation with Jeanne over that word. "I'm staying for a few days playing tourist and seeing the sights. I'll visit as soon as I get home," he lied. He had become a good liar these days. Without pausing to take another breath he said, "This call is costing you a fortune. I'll hang up now. Kiss the kids and say hi to Bob. Bye for now."

Once again he hung up without waiting for a reply. *What did I do, he thought holding his head. But what choice did I have? How could I tell her that her mother doesn't know her? What should I do now with this lie? Not a whole lie, though. This woman is a stranger to me, not the Jeanne I knew.* "I'm running out of strength to cope," he mumbled. "I can't be alone any longer," he said, feeling friendless.

Sam paced the room; wringing his hands and shaking his head. He sat down on the sofa, put the TV on, stared at the screen, jumped up and shut it off. He continued walking the floor, back and forth, as if waiting for something or someone. With eyes upward as if looking for help, he said with a sob in his voice, "I don't have anyone."

Suddenly a strange thought ensued. *Ramon, Dr. Gonzalez. He's a professional who appears to be a decent man. Maybe he can advise me. Dare I ask him? No, he'll be prejudiced considering his relationship with Jeanne. How can I think such a thing? Shows how desperate I am. A wave of nausea swept over him thinking of the two of them together.* "It's insane," he uttered. "But again..." Sam had adopted the habit of talking to himself when he was troubled.

The setting sun cast shadows upon the wall. A strong breeze swept through the open window causing the curtains to sway. He became aware of the changing temperature and shivered, shutting the window. The room was getting dark, and he had to turn on the lights. The action broke through his thoughts and in a voice raised in inflection, startling himself, he said, "I'm hungry."

-36-

Dr. Lopez introduced himself to Marguerite as their first session started. "Please have a seat in the reclining chair and unwind. I find people are more comfortable in this position."

He started with the usual questions -- name, address, date of birth.

"Marguerite Perez. 121-02 Bolivar Boulevard. I don't know my birth date."

"It's all right," he responded in a calm, quiet voice. "Sometimes a direct question triggers a response. Don't worry, we'll work at it."

She remained tense waiting for the treatment to start.

"Close your eyes and breathe deeply exhaling through your mouth," he said in a monotone. "My name is Hector Lopez and I will try to help you recall your former life. Keep breathing," he reiterated, "It helps you concentrate on me and not on your thoughts."

He continued with general conversation. He was born in a small town north of Caracas, he told her, attended university in the city, was married, had four children, and enjoyed helping people conquer their fears and problems. "I will keep this session short so as not to tire you out the first time." He never asked her to talk. He wanted her to listen to him and become accustomed to his voice.

The monotone pitch worked insofar as Marguerite relaxed and her mind became vacant for the first time in the past few days.

Dr. Lopez ended the session without putting her under or discussing anything special. "We will meet every other day for one week and see what happens."

Jeanne felt comfortable with Dr. Lopez and at last had a positive feeling. "Maybe this will work," she said to him.

*

At Marguerite's second session, Dr. Lopez started his treatment in earnest. "Look at this gold watch," he said as she settled down on the reclining chair. He spoke in a professional intonation while swinging the watch slowly in front of her. The watch had a plain cover, so she wouldn't be distracted with the time. "Concentrate on the movement and breathe deeply. Picture a favorite place in the woods with a nearby stream and pretty flowers all around. Forget the pressures of the day and concentrate on the surroundings of green grass, leafy trees and blue sky. Your eyes are getting heavy and you can't keep them open any longer. You can close them and when you do you will not feel anything from now on. You will listen to my instructions and reply to my questions. I will do nothing to harm or embarrass you. I promise," he continued in a soft pitched voice.

Marguerite's eyes were closed. Her hands open, palms up, shoulders down, feet falling to the side, the pose of a person in a completely restful place. Her even breathing indicated to Dr. Lopez that she was in a hypnotic state. He pricked the right forearm. She did not move.

"You are going to transfer your thoughts to include the past and go into the present."

Where are you?"

"In Dr. Lopez's office?"

"What is your name?"

She hesitated and said, "I'm not sure."

"Are you called Marguerite?"

"Yes."

"Are you called Jeanne?"

"Yes."

"You can't be two people. Who are you? There's no thinking," the doctor said. "Tell me the first thing that comes into your mind."

"Jeanne Golden."

"Who is Jeanne Golden?"

"Me."

"Then who is Marguerite?"

"I don't know. I thought I knew her, but now I'm not sure. Everyone says Jeanne and Marguerite are the same, but I think they are two people."

"What makes them two people?"

Jeanne started to squirm in the chair. She tried to open her eyes but couldn't.

"Where does Jeanne live?" the doctor asked, not pressing her to answer the question that made her uncomfortable.

"In New York!"

"And this woman, Marguerite?"

"Caracas."

"Jeanne, are you also Marguerite?"

"Yes," she said without hesitation. I used to be Jeanne in my other life. But now..."

"Do you like Marguerite?"

"Oh yes. She's free without obligations. She leads an exciting life. She's in love with a doctor. They dance. They sing. They go for walks on the beach. She loves her job..."

"How about Jeanne? Do you like her?"

"She's unhappy. She doesn't love her husband anymore. She outgrew him. He doesn't let her work and be independent." Her voice rose, her body stiffened. She started to tighten her grip on the chair.

"Jeanne, how about Sara?"

"Sara-- my child? I, I don't remember her," she said with tears running down her face.

Dr. Lopez, who was studying her movements, saw the change in her expression. Eyelids fluttering trying to open, brow creased in concentration, hands clenched, feet moving as opposed to the relaxed condition she was in just a few minutes ago. Upon seeing her anguish, he released her from the hypnotic state. As her eyes opened, she jumped up, rubbed her hands and arms as if to brush something from her." I feel very nervous and shaky. What happened? What did I say? Who am I?"

"We had a very successful morning," he said giving her a tissue. "We managed to break through some tough matters, but you need time for your subconscious to adjust to these findings. We'll discuss this tomorrow," he said kindly. "I did not want to see you every day, but I've changed my mind and feel back to back meetings will be beneficial. Go home, have a glass of wine, unwind, enjoy the evening, and I'll see you soon. By the way, you can call me at anytime. Don't worry," he said patting her arm, "You'll be fine."

"Thank you," she said in a soft voice, as she gathered her jacket and purse and left.

-37-

Once home, Marguerite puttered around the apartment too agitated to sit. She watered the plants even though they had their drinks the day before. She straightened the pillows on the couch, wiped the bathroom sink twice, swept the kitchen floor, dusted the living room and collapsed in exhaustion on the couch.

As if needing permission, she said, "Dr. Lopez suggested I should have a glass of wine," and poured herself a glass of Madeira. She closed her eyes and reflected about what she might have said to the doctor. When she finished the second glass, she went to the telephone and dialed the number in Massachusetts, closing her eyes to the ringing on the other end.

"Hello," a little girl answered. "Hello," she repeated when there was no response.

"Can I talk to your mother please?"

Marguerite was starting to feel dizzy and had to hold on to the table for support.

"Hello."

"Sara."

"Yes, may I help you?"

Marguerite, trembling, forced her voice to be strong and said, "I knew your mother"...

'My mother," Sara gasped. "My mother is dead."

"I, I knew her a long time ago..."

"Who are you? Why are you calling? When did you see her?"

"My name is Marguerite Perez. I knew her a long time ago," she repeated. "I don't know why I'm calling you." Marguerite was at a loss for words and didn't know how to continue. She took a gulp of wine and said in a meek voice, "I just wanted to hear your voice. I thought you might be able to help me. I'm sorry I bothered you."

"How did you get my number? What do you want?" Sara shouted.

Marguerite hung up totally confused. She collapsed on the floor crying and hugging her knees. The wine went directly to her head. She was suddenly dizzy and weak lacking any strength. The room was spinning. Bewildered and unsure of where she was she sat on the floor in a stupor trying to conjure up a picture of Sara but couldn't. All she heard was, "my mother is dead over and over," and the terrible anguish in her daughter's voice. "What did I do," she cried, caught up in her own torment.

The effects of the drink and the excitement of the call caused her body to give way. She lied on the floor, curled up in the fetal position, and passed out.

-38-

Sam took several tours of the city to pass the time, until Jeanne would come to him. He felt assured that she would remember him. He saw Caracas by day and Caracas by night. He took a boat ride and visited the museums. The art museum brought back memories of the times when he and Molly would roam the Metropolitan in New York. He smiled as he remembered looking at the Degas ballerina. *What a wonderful time we had in Washington, when we went to see the Degas exhibit. I wonder how she is,* he thought heaving a sigh. Although the museum had numerous treasures, it did not hold his interest anymore, and he left thinking he must make some decisions soon.

As the days passed, Sam felt defeated. *How long can I stay here? She doesn't know me and doesn't seem to be making an effort to see me.* Over lunch in the hotel cafe, he made the decision to go home. *I'll call Jeanne and give her my number in the event that she wants it. I'll visit Sara. It'll do us good to spend time together.* Pondering his plan, over coffee, he thought *I'll have to put on a good front for her. I can't let her know her mother is alive and doesn't know her. It'll break her heart.*

The phone was ringing when he returned to his room, still thinking of Sara. As if on the same wave length, he heard her voice as he picked up the receiver.

"Dad, the weirdest thing happened," she blurted out. "I got a call from a woman who said she knew Mom..."

"What are you saying? Who called you?" he interrupted.

"I was so excited when she said she knew my mother, I forgot her name. But it was Spanish sounding."

"What did she say?"

"She knew Mom a long a time ago and needed to talk to me. Then she hung up. What do you think that was all about?" In her usual brisk manner, she continued, "I was so upset, I couldn't sleep last night. I still can't shake the awful feeling of that call." Taking a breath, she realized there was no sound from the other end of the telephone. "Dad, are you there?"

"I'm here," Sam said slowly. The room was turning. He had to sit down. In a cold sweat, the ends of the hairline stuck to his neck. "I don't know what to say," he was finally able to mumble. "It probably was a prank from someone who knows why I'm here," he said in a lighter voice, trying to protect his child.

"What kind of a person would pull such a prank? If in fact it was a prank. It's eerie."

What kind of a person, indeed, he thought. *How dare she call Sara.*

"Dad, can you come home? -- I need to see you."

Having to talk to Sara forced the anger from forming. "My sentiments exactly," he said, and made up his mind, in an instant. "I'll leave at the end of the week and fly directly to Logan. I'll let you know the particulars. Sarie, my sweet, don't dwell. The person making that call is mean spirited and stupid," he spat. "There's all kinds of lunatics walking around."

"Sure Dad. Sure. I'm still haunted but feel a little better talking to you. I'm glad you'll be here soon. I love you."

"Me too, baby."

Sam hung up and immediately went to confront Jeanne.

-39-

Marguerite's third session started in the usual manner. She asked Dr. Lopez what ensued previously, and he said they would talk before she left. Being familiar with the procedure, she went under in a matter of minutes.

"How is Jeanne today?"

"O.K., I guess."

"Is Marguerite still around?"

"She's slowly going away. Jeanne is overpowering her. She needs to be with her child. She spoke to her daughter but didn't tell her she was her mother."

"What will happen to Marguerite?"

"She'll disappear here in Caracas. Jeanne will go home."

"What about Ramon?"

Jeanne started to cry. "I don't know." She clutched her fingers into fists. Her voice quivered. "I don't know."

"And Sam?" the doctor pushed on.

"I can't go back to him, she screamed. "I can't. I don't know him."

He pushed on despite her agitation. "Were you happy with Sam?"

"Happy. I can't remember."

The doctor was quiet, giving her time to think.

"We were once happy. Then I don't know what happened. We grew apart. Oh!" she stopped talking and began rocking back and forth. She seemed to be looking back into time, "The affairs, the confrontations, the accusations. The terrible scenes!" She stood up, with her eyes still closed shaking her fist at the air. "We lived a lie."

Seeing how upset she was and sensing the turmoil within her, he said, "Maguerite, you'll wake up at the count of three."

She opened her eyes, staring at Dr. Lopez as if she didn't know who he was.

"Here's a tissue," he said. "Can I get you a glass of water?"

Marguerite looked around, trying to get a sense of where she was. She was slowly coming to herself, as she saw the familiar setting. The dark walnut paneling, void of any decorations, complemented the tan leather sofa and chairs. She started to feel warm and protected in this cocoon, until the doctor started to talk.

"You are Jeanne aren't you?"

"I am..."

"You talk of Jeanne in the third person. You never say me. You always refer to Jeanne as someone else."

She ignored him. "I'm starting to remember isolated incidents. I don't know how I got here or why? But I can see me and Sam at home. I was just there. We don't talk much. I can't see Sara. It upsets me not to be able to know her or her children."

"You're remembering Sam easier because you've seen him. Perhaps if you see a picture of Sara it will all come back. What did you talk to her about?"

"Nothing! I chickened out and hung up. But I think I may have upset her." Jeanne played with the crumpled tissue. "I told her I knew her mother a long time ago."

"That's not far from the truth," he said. "You did know her then and must get to know her again. I think that you have to meet with Sam and see what happens."

"I'm scared," she said leaning forward on the chair. "I don't know if I have the strength. What will I say?"

The kindly doctor said, "Perhaps you both can meet here with me being a sort of mediator. Would you like that?"

"Oh could you? I need your stability. I feel like I could curl up and hide. Remembering the past is hard. Facing the future will be harder still. Who will I have to hurt? Will I ever be me again?"

"Who is me?" he asked.

-40-

Sam rang Marguerite's doorbell with such determination that he did not take his finger off.

Opening the door she said, "What's going on?

He stormed into her apartment, eyes blazing with anger. "I should ask you what's going on? How dare you call Sara and scare her? Are you crazy?"

"I didn't mean anything? I thought I would be able to talk to her. I couldn't."

"If you don't know her, she's mine. Don't try to contact her again." Sam shook his finger menacingly at her.

"Mr. Golden. Uh -- Sam please listen to me. Let's talk."

"There's no talking. You chose to be a stranger. I have nothing to say."

"Please, please," she said looking straight into his eyes. Her own filled with tears, lips quivering. "I'm involved with hypnosis and am trying so hard to remember. Please."

She looked so pathetic, so tired, so pale. He tried to control himself. "So talk," he said in a belligerent tone, still standing in the same aggressive position; hands clenched at his side, feet planted firmly. He looked like he might hit her.

Jeanne pointed to one of the striped chairs. "Let's sit." She sat down; he remained standing with an irritated look. Always the consummate hostess, she said in a voice smooth as honey, "Can I get you something to drink? I have iced tea. Do you still like iced tea with sugar?"

"Sure..." Sam almost fell over. His stance loosened. "You remember me?"

"I, what?"

"Don't you realize you said, "Do I still like iced tea?"

"I did?"

"Don't you know what you said?

Jeanne was stunned. Her forehead wrinkled into a frown and a puzzled look on her face, not fully comprehending the situation.

"Jeanne, don't you see what's happening. You are starting to recollect things. We need some support here. Maybe we can call your hypnosis doctor. He might be able to help you recall other things, now that there is a break through and things are fresh in your mind."

"Don't rush me. I need time. Too much pressure," she said playing with the lace curtains as she looked out of the window. *What's happening to me,* she thought holding her head as if in pain. *Am I hearing voices in my head or am I going crazy?*

Sam put his hands on her shoulders and felt her give an involuntary shake. He left his hands on her and said, "Jeanne, Jeanne, My Jeanne. Come home. Come back to me and Sara."

At the mention of Sara she turned towards him. "Don't you think I want to know my own child? Do you think I am some sort of a monster? I'm not. I care. But I can't.

'Please go. I need to think," she yelled. "My head is killing me," her tone changing to a whisper.

"Go ahead and think. You lie down, I won't bother you. I'll just sit quietly. I have no place to go anyway."

-41-

Lina and her brother were one year apart in age and had always had a very close relationship. They made sure that despite their busy schedules, they would meet at least once a month. During their monthly lunch in the Alcazar Restaurant, down the block from Ramon's office, Lina asked her brother, "By the way, how's Marguerite? You don't bring her around anymore."

"She's fine, although she's no longer Marguerite. She now knows she's really Jeanne."

"You mean she remembers her past life?" she said, shocked, holding the fork in her hand.

"No. But her subconscious under hypnosis revealed her to be Jeanne and she accepts it. She doesn't remember her husband even after seeing him."

"For real or does she just want you?" Lina said looking straight at Ramon.

He was weary. "Why are you so distrustful? What did she do to you? You don't even know her," he said annoyed.

"I don't mean to be so negative. I have bad feelings -- that's all, and I always want to protect you," she answered in a soft voice.

"I'm a big boy now and can protect myself."

Trying to calm him, she said quietly, "Why not leave some distance between you and her? Don't see her for a while and let her go on with the treatment with no interference. Maybe your presence is keeping her from her past life."

Lina took Ramon's hands in hers across the table and smiled at him. "Give it a try. Advice, from an older sister who cares." To herself she said *and maybe she'll get the message and leave.*

Ramon continued eating his favorite dish, fried shrimps, the house specialty, without comment. Taking a long drink of his second martini, and eating both of the olives to empty the glass, he looked at Lina and said, "Perhaps you are right. You and I are usually on the same wave length, so maybe it'll work."

The meal ended with their obligatory flan and a hug. "Call you tomorrow," she waved getting into a cab.

In his car, Ramon thought, *I'd better get this over with and go directly to Jeanne. Funny, I still have trouble thinking of her as Jeanne. Marguerite fits her so much better. Less formal! Younger!*

*

Grinning, Sam opened the door with a cup in his hand, holding a dish towel, looking as if he belonged there. Ramon's smile turned into a scowl. Shaking his head he turned and walked away.

"Who's there Sam?" she said coming out of the bedroom.

"Wrong apartment, come have coffee. There's delicious cake with it."

Ramon slammed the outer door so hard, the glass panel shattered.

Jeanne spent the rest of the afternoon with Sam talking about the city, the weather, and world events. She had collected herself and was quieter now. They even shared a pizza for dinner.

Having not heard from Ramon all day, Jeanne called him with no response other than the machine. She left several messages. He never returned them. She called him again and again. "I hope Ramon's all right," she said. "This is so not like him."

"He's probably busy at the hospital," Sam hinted and encouraged her to go to Boston. "It'll do you good to get back to your home ground and off foreign soil."

-42-

During the subsequent hypnotic treatments, she started to have flashbacks, but they did not lead to anything of real consequence. They did refresh her memory somewhat. She was more bewildered than ever. "I can see my home," Jeanne told Dr. Lopez, while in her sleeplike state. "It's a white house with a red door. There's a very pretty garden, with lots of flowers. I loved reading in the early morning surrounded by the beautiful colors and fragrances."

"Who lives with you?"

"I can't see anyone, only the house and the garden."

She spent many hours at home reliving the scene in her mind, trying to see who shared her house, to no avail.

On another occasion, when she was questioned about a memory from childhood, Jeanne spoke of taking her child to school for the first time. Dr. Lopez meant her own childhood, but somehow she confused the issue. "I can't see her clearly."

"How do you know it's a her?"

"I don't know. I can't see her face, but I am holding her hand."

Sometimes she didn't remember what she said while under. The doctor had to tell her during their discussion after the session. This made her very confused. "How can I know something while hypnotized and forget it when I'm released?"

"This is part of the process. I think it will all fall into place, if you just have some patience."

The next day Jeanne said, "Doctor, I've decided to go to Boston to meet Sara."

"Do you think it's wise? We're starting to break through the muddle."

"I feel I have to go. I'll be with Sam. It'll be all right. He'll take me to see Sara. I need that now. You've helped me so very much. How can I ever thank you?

'By the way, have you seen Ramon?" Jeanne said twisting her necklace.

"Not recently. Everything O.K.?"

"Sure. Look, I'll keep in touch and fill you in on how I am progressing with the treatment at home. I'll miss you and your kind ways," Jeanne said, giving him a hug.

*

Upon leaving the therapist, Jeanne headed straight for Ramon's office and what she hoped wouldn't be a confrontation but a misunderstanding. "He's not here," Maria said. "He took a few days off. I don't know where he went. His associate is covering for him."

Jeanne escaped to the street. Her face was red as though dyed. She was filled with anger, and started to run. When finally her breath gave way, she slowed to a walk. *How can he do this to me? Why? What's happened?* Her mood changed from rage to a feeling of uncertainty. A car's honking horn broke through her concentration. Jeanne was so focused on Ramon and his unexplained absence that she almost walked into the path of a car. This near miss calmed her immediately and she headed home.

She called Lina. "Where is Ramon?" she asked very directly.

"Why he went on a vacation. Didn't he tell you?" Lina asked in a voice dripping with innocence. "I thought everything was going along smoothly between you both."

"It was. But now I don't know. It's foreign to me that he would just go away like that. Did he go alone?"

"I really can't discuss that." She hoped this vague answer would further confuse Jeanne. "Maybe you both need some time and space."

As she hung up, Jeanne thought *it really is time for me to go home. I thought I knew him and his feelings towards me, but I guess I didn't. Do I know my feelings towards him now?*

-43-

Sam and Jeanne checked into the Copley Plaza in the heart of Boston.

"I'll be right next door if you need anything," Sam said. He had not left her side since his encounter at the door. He hoped she would get used to him and become dependent or better still realize she loved him after all.

Sam called Sara to tell her he was in town and would see her the next day. He timed his visit so that she would be alone.

"Sara, sit. I have to talk to you," he said after they exchanged hugs and pleasantries about his trip, the family, and the fact that he was back home in the United States. They were always able to talk. They related better than she did with her mother. Father and daughter sat opposite each other at the plain wooden table in the pretty country kitchen holding cups of coffee. They even shared their passion of consuming the caffeinated drink in large quantities.

Sam put his cup down and said, "I don't know how to say this, so I'll be direct. Mom's alive."

Sara's cup dropped, breaking as it hit the table, the dark fluid running down, staining the parquet floor. Her hands flew up to her wide open mouth. She gasped for air and jumped out of her chair, pounding her father on his chest. "What are you saying? Alive? How? When?"

He took her hands and hugged her shaking body. Her body trembled with such force and her face so ashen that he held her tightly, afraid she would faint. "It's all right. Cry it out. I couldn't tell you before," he said gently patting her hair. "There was nothing to tell. You would be hurt. She didn't remember anything. But now, she's been under hypnosis and things are starting to unravel. She wants to see you."

Backing away facing him, she said incredulously, wiping her eyes, "It was Mom who called me that day wasn't it? How could she do that to me and why didn't she tell me who she was?"

"Don't look back. Let's go get reacquainted."

"I can't go. I can't face her, if she doesn't know me. I won't..."

"Sure you can. You'll see it's just Mom."

*

Since Sam told her he was bringing their daughter to see her, she was a nervous wreck. Preoccupied, she wondered if she would recognize her daughter. She walked the length and width of the room biting her nails while she waited for them. She straightened the bedspread and fluffed the pillows for the tenth time. Jeanne absentmindedly rearranged the two chairs around the circular table near the window "I will not cry. I will not cry," she repeated, trying to calm down. She combed her hair, pinned it back, recombed it, and decided to leave it loose.

Hearing the knock she smoothed her hair once more, checked her face in the mirror, stalling for time. Finally taking a deep breath, she opened the door. She remained still as if frozen to the floor staring at the lovely girl in front of her. In a moment Jeanne absorbed her daughter with the straight back, tender pink mouth, and blonde highlighted hair twisted into one long braid.

Sara wavered then bolted with outstretched arms to Jeanne, almost knocking her over. "Mommy, Mommy," she cried hugging her mother so hard Jeanne winced. Hugging her back she hesitated for a split second. Sara felt the uncertainty and backed off. Holding her head and pulling at her hair, she cried, "You really don't know me, your own child, do you?"

"Honey, I..."

"How could you forget your flesh and blood? How could you?" she asked. "You, who taught me the meaning of family. Where is it? We vanished on the beach like a lost coin?"

Jeanne clutched Sara to her with a strength she didn't know she had. "I'm trying..."

Sara broke free and sobbed, "Trying? Bullshit. It's not enough. I lost you once. How many times do I have to lose my mother?"

-44-

When Ramon saw Sam at Marguerite's apartment, he assumed he had lost her. He interpreted the happy look on Sam's face and the familiar manner in which he answered the door to mean that Marguerite chose Sam over him. He ran away a defeated man. *I need to get out of here.* He headed home.

As he drove out of the city he thought, *I started to lose Marguerite when she became Jeanne. But I'll always think of her as Marguerite no matter what name she uses.* He agonized over the fact that it was he who suggested hypnosis in the first place. *She was happy with me and afraid of learning about her past. What a dope. Couldn't leave well enough alone, could I?*

*

Ramon fled to the mountains of Venezuela, seeking solitude. An avid fisherman, he spent many hours alone standing in hip boots in the rolling waters of the stream, a run off from the natural waterfalls of the mountain area. The twisting and turning of the water was like the turmoil he was encountering. *What should I do* he thought, reeling in a large trout. *Should I put up a fight for her like this fish has done with me? Or should I acquiesce and let her go back to her family like my friend the fish, who is finally submitting without resistance, and letting me catch him?*

The lush jungle-state of the woods, the leafy trees, thick grass and wild flowers, the cacophony of birds, together with the sounds of the water breaking against the rocks, created a cocoon for Ramon. Even though his mind worked overtime trying to adjust to losing, his body relaxed. The lines along his face smoothed under his newly acquired tan. The sun warmed his body as he fished in the water.

He cooked and ate the bounty of the creek alongside the small fire he put together. He slept in a sleeping bag under the dark sky illuminated by the multitude of stars and a full moon. The solitude did him good. He made his decision. *When I get back home, I'll fight for her.* "I won't be a quitter," he shouted to the night. "I love her whether she is Jeanne or Marguerite, and I'll be dammed if I'll go down without a battle."

*

Ramon returned to Caracas after two weeks in the mountains and went directly to Jeanne's apartment. Her downstairs neighbor reported that Ms. Perez had moved out.

"Moved where?"

"I don't know. She was with a man. They took her things, said good-bye and left."

He went home and listened to the answering machine. There were several messages from Jeanne -- but no information. "Ramon where are you? Are you all right? Call me." He called Maria. "Any messages?"

"Ms. Perez was here looking for you and left in a huff when she didn't find you."

Ramon called Dr. Lopez, and without any cordial greeting blurted, "Where is Jeanne?"

"Gone to the United States! Didn't she tell you?"

"We had a falling out."

"No wonder she asked me if I had heard from you. She went to meet her daughter, with Sam..."

"Son of a bitch," he said as he hung up the telephone without hearing the end of the sentence. "At least someone will be happy," he sobbed throwing himself onto the couch. "I failed."

-45-

Jeanne started her therapy with Dr. Birnbaum, referred by Dr. Lopez. While in a hypnotic state he had her talk about her current life, easy things, to establish their relationship. He then directed many questions about her past. Dr. Birnbaum set up specific scenarios describing happy events that might have applied to her.

"I see you in the kitchen preparing a holiday meal for Thanksgiving. Do you like Thanksgiving?"

"I love this holiday."

"Who shares this day with you?"

"My family and some close friends always spend the holidays with me."

"Are you famous for any special delicacies?"

"I make a traditional feast - turkey with the usual trimmings. I bake all the desserts. Sara loves my pumpkin pie with vanilla ice cream. Brianna helps me serve the dessert. She's very serious about this chore." Jeanne emitted a chuckle, which was very rare for her while in this sleep-like state.

"Jeanne, how do you celebrate your birthday? Does Sam give you any special gifts?"

"I'm not sure she whispered."

"How about Sara and your grandchildren?"

"Sara is great. We don't live near each other, so I go there for a few days. The kids make me cards, gifts and a special birthday cake. It's fun, she muttered."

As Jeanne answered all of the doctor's questions, she did so in a monotone bereft of feeling. The only change in her tone was when Sam's name was mentioned.

In a subsequent session, the doctor delved into her marriage. He sensed her discomfort in this area, and deliberately stayed away from it, but now was the time for confrontation.

"Jeanne, did you have a happy marriage?" He waited a few minutes and when there was no answer he asked, "Were you a devoted couple?"

"I don't know." Jeanne's expression changed to a glare. She wrinkled her brow as if in displeasure. She squirmed in the chair, clenching the arms, which the doctor recognized as her usual sign for, "I've had enough."

When she returned to a normal state, after coming out of the hypnotic state, Dr. Birnbaum remarked, "During the session you never mention Sam. Your memories are all about Sara."

"I don't know him. I don't remember him and I don't care." Her voice took on an acrid tone. "I do not see my husband. I can tell you something about him, but I don't know him. You say he's Sam Golden -- fine. I accept that, but I only know him from now."

"You are purposely blanking him out of your mind, you know. By this time there must be some memory. You do recall other things and other people. Do you think it's because you don't want to go back with him?" the doctor offered in a straight forward way.

Jeanne looked around the office, concentrating on the walnut framed diploma from NYU Medical School, the certificate confirming the completion of his psychiatric residency, and the Diplomate Accreditation Certificate hanging on the wall behind Dr. Birnbaum's desk.

"Jeanne, be honest, at least with me. Remember this conversation goes no further."

"I don't know if I'm honest with myself or even if I've ever been," she despaired.

"Think it over. We'll talk again," he promised, shaking her hand good bye.

-46-

Jeanne moved from the Copley Plaza to a small motel near Sara's home. She planned to stay in the area for awhile, at least until she completed the course of therapy. The cost of the motel was almost half of the upscale hotel, which fit her pocketbook. She also wanted to be near to the family to order to become reacquainted. Sam followed along like an obedient puppy dog.

Sam made every effort to win Jeanne over. He attended to her every need. First thing in the morning he would call her with a schedule for the day. "I'll drive you to the therapist. I'll wait and we'll have lunch together. Then we can go to the children."

For the first few days she agreed, and was grateful for the support. The constant togetherness, though, seemed to grate on her nerves. Not wanting to offend, she continued this routine. *My usual pattern is pleasing everyone.*

Sam assumed things were going so well between them that he planned a romantic evening. They started with dinner at a posh restaurant. Dinner was just the beginning of his design. "We need time alone and deserve the luxury," he told Jeanne. The restaurant was ornately adorned with mauve silk wall covering and matching draperies and tablecloths. The tables were elegantly set with the finest crystal stemware and white and gold dinner service. A small floral centerpiece completed the setting. As they sipped their champagne cocktails, they looked the perfect couple. Very pleased with the situation, Sam boasted, "You and I together are just great. I'm so happy that I found you and we're together again."

Jeanne flinched as she emptied the crystal flute and started on her second drink. "I think I'm going to look for a part-time job," she blurted. "I saw a sign looking for help in the window of a ladies upscale boutique down the block from the doctor's office."

'You should relax and get better. Anyway, what do you know about the styles and clothes in such a fancy shop?"

Ignoring the putdown, she focused on the seafood crepe, and found herself apologizing as usual. "I can learn. I was always a good shopper and I know what women like," she said using a more confident tone. "Besides I need the money. The rent is a fortune."

"Not necessary. I can and will provide. We have savings and there's my pension. It'll be enough. We can spend the days together, lunch, maybe a museum, and anyway soon we'll be back home."

"But it's something I want to do..."

Interrupting, his voice rising, he hissed, "With me, you never worked before, so why now? Was your doctor friend happy that you clerked in that menial job in the supermarket?"

Seeing the look on her face, wide eyes, teeth clenched, putting her fork down so gently, he spoke before she did. "Look honey, I'm only interested in your welfare. Have fun like other ladies. Go to shows, shop, play with the kids."

"Thank you very much. I can amuse myself without instructions from you and by the way I'll work if I want to. The past is gone. Now is today! She got up abruptly, "I'm going to the ladies room." To herself she said, *I'll have a good cry since I don't know what else to do. I'm so mixed up.*

Sam downed the last of the champagne thinking *what did I do that was so wrong? I'll smooth things out when she gets back. There's the rest of the night ahead of us. She'll calm down. Work, humph, what's she thinking?*

115

-47-

After a few stilted meetings between Jeanne and Sara, an open truce developed. Sara mellowed as she spent time with her mother and saw how hard she was trying. Each day brought new memories for Jeanne. She felt good that things were coming back.

Jeanne was determined to make a concerted effort to call Sara every day. "Good morning," Jeanne chirped in an upbeat voice.

"Hi Mom, had a good night?"

"Great. Slept like a baby. What's on your agenda for today? Can we get together?

"Sure," Sara answered with a smile in her voice. "Meet you at the Palace Cafe which is only a few blocks from Dr. Birnbaum's office."

Jeanne heaved a sigh. "Dad can go to your house and wait for the children. We'll spend the afternoon --just the two of us."

During their lunch of shrimp salad and iced tea; they chatted about the usual things, the weather, the children, or a television program they both enjoyed. A real camaraderie took place. Jeanne shared the current results of her therapy. It made Sara happy to hear that her mother was remembering more and more.

"Mom, what about Dad? You never talk about him. What's up?"

"Nothing -- really. I don't seem to remember much about us. I don't know why." She buttered a biscuit, and mustered all of her nerve. "Dr. Birnbaum thinks I blot him out subconsciously because I want to. I recall him in the singular, but still not as a couple. I know about Daddy and his family, how he grew up, where they lived. Things like that. But I still don't know anything about us."

"Dad loves you so much. How can't you know him?"

Jeanne didn't answer. She ate, focusing on the salad.

"Don't ignore me like you did with Daddy!" Sara was furious. She stabbed a chunk of shrimp. "I saw how you shut him out. He came home from work, ate and puttered in the garden until dark. Then you read or knitted or whatever and both watched television. There was no intimate communication, no affection. Why; you never even sat next to him."

"What are you saying? I was such an ogre? A cold hearted monster?"

"No, not a monster, but cold hearted towards him. Did you love him?"

Jeanne put her coffee cup down and looked at her daughter whose eyes held so much pain. "Sara what does a child know about her parents' relationship? You only saw the outside. You always were closer to your father than to me. I thought it was the usual mother- daughter- oil and-vinegar mix. But now I think that we are very much alike. You'll understand when someday I tell you about my former life."

-48-

Opening the envelope from the American Medical Association, Ramon read the enclosed invitation, embossed on the finest stationery.

TO: *Ramon Pena Gonzalez, M.D.*

         Caracas, Venezuela

You are cordially invited to be a guest speaker at the annual convention of the American Medical Association.

LOCATION: *Copley Plaza Hotel*

           Boston, Massachusetts

TOPIC: *International Medical Ethics*

"Boston," he cried aloud. "How eerie, although muy fantastico." *A definite sign that I should follow her, he thought. I'm glad my course, Medical Ethics, at the Medical College and my publication in the Journal of Medicine paid off with recognition from the AMA.*

Now, how will I go about finding Jeanne? I had better get used to calling her Jeanne when I get to America. Quickly answering the invitation, he thought, *I only remember her daughter's name, Sara. She lives somewhere in Massachusetts.* He racked his brain trying to recall anything he could about Jeanne's family. Nothing! Finally he thought of Jeff Atlas, the Private Investigator.

"Mr. Atlas, Dr. Gonzalez here. I'm a friend of Jeanne Golden."

"Certainly, Doctor. What can I do for you?"

"I'm trying to locate the Goldens in a most urgent matter. Would you have a phone number or address? I think she's with her daughter?"

"How are they? Hope all is well. Yes, I have the Golden's home phone number and address in New York. Nothing about their child!"

Ramon thanked him and called Jeanne's home. What luck! The message gave a forwarding phone number. Pondering the issue of calling, he decided to go unannounced and see what would happen. He contacted a buddy, a guy he played cards with. Marco was a computer whiz. Using the internet he was able to match an address to the phone number.

It's a good thing I keep my passport up to date, he thought, as he waited to board the United Airlines plane. Ramon was on his way.

-49-

Jeanne agonized over her decision to take a sales associate job. Sam's words echoed in her mind- *what do you know about clothes in a fancy store?*

During their morning chat, Jeanne asked Sara, "What do you think of my going to work?"

"What a great idea Mom. Doing what?"

"Sales, at the Excelsior Boutique."

"Oh boy! It's a classy store. The clothes are fabulous and expensive. You'll be able to get me a discount, won't you?" she laughed. When do you start?"

"Am I qualified?" Jeanne asked, ignoring the question.

"Qualified, why not? What's there to know? You're very familiar with fashion. You always dress well and look very put together. You taught me to dress didn't you? And - you were the shopping queen." Giggling, she said "Remember? You never worked, just shopped."

Jeanne felt a sharp pain, like a stab in her heart. What a putdown, she thought. That's all I was good for, shopping?

Getting no response, Sara asked, "Mom are you O.K.?"

"Sure. Dad thought perhaps I should wait." She didn't want to tell Sara her father's reaction. Jeanne walked on eggs not wanting to antagonize her daughter. Sara and Sam were so close, she didn't want to talk about him afraid that she wouldn't understand and become belligerent.

"What for? You'll stay with me. You can't stay in a motel forever. Wait a minute, what about New York? If you get a job aren't you going home?"

"I love being near you, Bob, and the children. I've been away for so long. I have decided to make Massachusetts my home. I even looked at an apartment. It's real cute. A bedroom, a living room, and kitchen; and not far from the store. I appreciate your offer, but you deserve your privacy. Two women in the same kitchen, as the saying goes, is not a good mix."

Hesitatingly, Sara asked, "And Dad?"

"You'll have to ask him. For the time being it's for me. We'll see later on."

Not knowing what else to say, Sara said, "Uh, O.K., I guess. Good luck with the job and let me know about the discount."

Jeanne smiled and thought, *shows what's important; doesn't it? Discounts are always essential to us girls.* She laughed and a twinkle returned to her eyes, "No generation gap here."

-50-

Jeanne and Sam had dinner at a small local café. She suggested it, realizing that Sara and her family needed time alone. After a glass of Chardonnay, Jeanne broached the subject again. This time she was definite, having had her ego boosted by her daughter's confidence. She took a long deep breath. "Sam, I got the job. I start on Tuesday." She paused... "I have to tell you something else. I rented an apartment." A suggestion of a smile showed her relief, finally able to let go of that information.

"What! Are you nuts? I told you it wasn't necessary to go to work and an apartment..." Sputtering he said, "Where? Why? Why didn't you ask me before...?"

"It's for me. I need my independence." Afraid of losing her nerve, she took a sip of wine, raised her voice, and in a defiant tone shouted, "I cannot and will not have you keep me back any longer. I've been on my own for sometime now and you know what, I like it." She held onto the glass for something to do as she tried to calm down. Never one for confrontation, this left her quivering. She didn't want to fight, just to get her point across.

Sam was stunned at her outburst. "When did I ever do anything to keep you back? Didn't you go to book clubs, PTA, volunteer. I even gave you a free rein with the credit card to buy whatever you wanted." Almost like an afterthought, he added, "And how about Marty? Did I hold you back from that affair?"

Jeanne gasped as if slapped in the face, got up so quickly the chair fell over. Her face became a light shade of red, almost as if she had added pink blush to her cheeks. Leaving the chair lay on its side on the floor, she screamed, "You've got some nerve bringing that up? Who do you think you are? Mister- holier- than- thou!"

A quietness fell across the restaurant. All eyes turned to this scene. The waiter came running and put the chair right side up and asked, "Is everything all right?" Jeanne was ashamed, realizing what she must have sounded like. Sitting down she lowered her voice but still spoke in an livid tone almost a hiss. "Best for me, or best for you? After all these years you don't know anything about me. Who am I? What do I want? You only know what I look like; a fifty-eight year old bleached blonde with blue eyes. Do you even know how tall I am or how much I weigh?" She took a deep breath and wondered where this came from. She drank the water in front of her in one gulp, holding the glass with a shaking hand.

"Who are you? You're my wife. That's who you are. I supported you -- gave you everything. You wanted for nothing." Sam became more belligerent, pointing his finger at her. "Don't give me any baloney that I kept you back. Back from what? You had a home, family, friends. What more could you want? And independent? I never kept tabs on you. You went where you wanted and what happened? You betrayed my trust. And now blame me!"

Interrupting him, Jeanne stood, pushed the chair away and said, "And..."

Sam softened his tone. "I don't know what you want," he pleaded.

"That my dear Sam is the problem," Jeanne proclaimed as she walked away. She turned around and said, "By the way I'm 5 feet 5 and weigh 136 pounds. Not bad for a fiftyish wife, mother and grandmother."

Sam remained at the table staring at the empty space where his wife just sat.

-51-

Ramon smiled as he stepped from the plane onto American soil. *I'm another step closer to Marguerite ... Jeanne.* He crossed his fingers and thought, *we'll be together soon.* He headed straight to the Copley Plaza, in the heart of Boston. As he entered the lobby with its brightly polished marble floors and plush furniture surrounded with vases of fresh flowers, he remembered that the AMA Convention was always held in an elaborate hotel.

Ramon's presentation about Medical Ethics was well received after several doctors told him how interesting his lecture was. The moral principled subject was complex and gave rise to many arguments. He presented a case where a doctor had a personal relationship with a female patient. This doctor used the patient's vulnerability to have her depend on him, leading to a romantic escapade. He concluded with, "Was this within the realm of ethical behavior?"

The questions and answers, from the audience, brought many different reactions. Was she hurt by the relationship? Did the doctor's action hinder her recovery? Was he malicious or kind? Would the end result justify the behavior? There were more questions than answers, but each one led to further discussion.

It remained inappropriate for a psychiatrist to have a patient/doctor relationship. Was it appropriate for an internist? There were no conclusive answers; many opinions. The majority concluded, however, that it was incorrect and outside of the bounds of ethical behavior for a physician.

I myself wrestled with this dilemma when I started to have feelings for Jeanne, he said to himself, as he listened to the repartee from his fellow doctors. *I knew what happened between me and Jeanne was unethical; actions of patient and doctor. I also knew that I could probably lose my professional standing. In my heart of hearts I knew it was wrong, yet I convinced myself I did the right thing. I told myself I was helping her. I was good for her. Wasn't I? Or was it good for me?*

The doctor collected his notes, and as he started to leave the podium, he was sure no matter how wrong his actions might have been, he had been good for her and she had been good for him.

The workshops in the afternoon of the last day of the convention were of no interest to Ramon. He said his good-byes at lunch, checked out, and headed towards Burlington.

*

Ramon rang the bell with trepidation. Visualizing the picture Sam had showed Jeanne, he realized it was Sara who opened the door. Not wanting to appear forward, he didn't acknowledge her. "Good afternoon. My name is Ramon Gonzalez. Is Mrs. Golden in?"

"What do you want with her?" Sara asked, clutching the door.

"I'm a friend from Caracas. I'm here for a few days and just want to say hello."

"Sorry. She's not here." The tone was definite.

"When will she be back?"

"I'm not at liberty to say," she answered and started to close the door.

"Please. I've come a long way and would like to see her. We really are friends you know."

His soft persistent manner caused her to pause.

"Be kind enough to ask her to call me. I'm staying at the Copley Plaza. I'll be in Boston for a few days."

His gentlemanly manner and large brown eyes silently pleading with her, broke her resistance. "I'll tell her but I don't promise anything."

"Thank you so much. Your mother tried so hard to remember you. I'm glad you found each other."

Sara closed the door, wondering what kind of relationship existed between this charming man and her mother. *He sure is good looking.* She got the distinct impression he was more than a friend. She shook her head, trying not to picture them together. *He should know he's at the same hotel she just left. What a coincidence.*

-52-

The sun began to set as evening approached. The thought of the stranger at the door continued as Sara started preparations for dinner. She put the water in for pasta- her children's favorite. Setting the table by rote she pondered; *what did my mother do all those months when she didn't remember who she was? Was she with him? She belongs to my father not another man. Should I tell her he was here?*

As she broke the spaghetti into the boiling water, Sam came in and kissed his daughter on the cheek. "What's for dinner sweetie?"

Smiling at her father she said, "Spaghetti and Meatballs."

"Smells wonderful! Is Mom here yet?"

"Not yet." Some inner sense urged her to keep the visit to herself. *I wonder how Dad would react? Better not take the chance.*

The ring of the telephone interrupted her reverie. "Mom, where are you?"

"Don't hold dinner for me. I'm stuck here. We have a customer who's spending a ton of money but is very annoying," Jeanne whispered with a smile in her voice. "She bought a pair of Prada sandals and is looking at a Versace sweater. Good commission. Since it'll be some time before I can leave, I'll go right home. Talk to you later."

Sounding like a robot with no animation, Sara said, "Mom, be careful."

Sara pondered the situation and tried to come to a decision, as she served her family. *I don't know what to do.*

"Sara, you forgot my meatballs," Sam said as she sat down. "What's the matter?"

Trying to introduce some levity she said, "Sorry. Have an extra to make up for my boo-boo."

With her fingers Brianna took one strand of spaghetti at a time and slurped it into her mouth. Concentrating on the task at hand, she asked, "Mommy who was the man who rang the bell? What did he want? You talked a long time. Did you tell him Daddy was working?"

Sara held her breath, her fork suspended in mid air on its way to her mouth, anticipating a response from her father. Sam was listening to Jeremy talk about his softball game, and seemed unaware of what the conversation was about. She wiped Brianna's face. "Don't talk with a mouth full, honey." She wanted to make sure there was no more talk about the visitor. She looked at Sam. "Dad what did you do today? You were out for a few hours."

Sam told her he went to the movies but continued talking with his grandson. She was quite relieved that the awkward moment passed without a problem.

*

As she prepared for bed, she still hadn't come to a decision. *Maybe if I talked with my mother, I could casually ask if she made friends during "that" phase of her life.* She phoned Jeanne before she lost her nerve. As she dialed, she caressed the porcelain statue on the nightstand. It was a young smiling girl wearing a blue dress and matching hat with a large brim, holding a small white dog. Her mother had given her this figurine on her sixteenth birthday just after her beloved dog Sandy had died. She now realized how thoughtful her mother had been.

Before Sara could start the conversation, Jeanne glowed, "I've had such a busy day, I'm beat! But I'm enjoying the job so much. I love the work and they love me. For the first time I feel important. I'm happy. And honey, an added bonus is we're together. It means so much to me. I've been through a terrible ordeal these past months and sure am glad they're over."

Hearing her mother sound so happy with her newly found importance, Sara remembered how her mother had instilled the need to be independent in her child. Jeanne had encouraged her to be an avid reader and to enjoy the vistas it opened for her. She took Sara to weekly piano lessons and helped her appreciate fine music. The need for higher education was promoted from childhood and continued until her graduation from Sarah Lawrence College. How was she repaying her mother for the opportunities afforded her? By sneaking and lying? By begrudging her a friend or God forbid a lover? But she couldn't help it. She was doing what she needed to do.

Sara made her mind up not to tell her mother about the visitor from

Venezuela. *He'll go back home thinking she doesn't care and that'll be the end of it. She'll be able to concentrate on going back with Dad without any interference from an outsider.*

Relieved that she took a stand, she read for a few minutes and promptly fell asleep.

For a while, she slept fitfully. Thoughts of whether she did right wandered through her mind. She woke during the night *thinking who am I to interfere in someone's life? Can I hide him from her? Should I? Would I like my child to determine my future?* Trying not to wake Bob, she put on her night light, and tried to clear her head, to no avail. *But on the other hand, she's my mother and I need my mother with my father, not some stranger.*

Flickers of light crept through the blinds. The long night came to an end. As the sun rose, it looked like a beautiful day. She got up to start her daily routine, looked in the mirror and said, "I look like shit."

*

Ramon also spent a restless night. He called Sara's house in the morning. Getting no answer he left a message on the voice mail. "Please have Jeanne call me at my hotel." His tone was curt and not as pleasant as it was the day before. He had a feeling Jeanne's daughter did not give her his message. She had acted distant and cold. *I'll have to find another avenue to try to locate mi amor.* He slipped into his native language without realizing it.

He had breakfast at the hotel's coffee shop. The cruller washed down with hot coffee made him feel somewhat better. He refused a second cup and thought, *one thing wrong with this country is its coffee.*

He needed to think and decided to take a walk to resolve how he could find Jeanne. As he walked his eyes gazed at the windows of the many different shops along the street. What a pretty window, he thought, when he came to the Excelsior Boutique.

-53-

Sara and Bob were out to dinner and Sam was the baby sitter. After many card games of spit, casino, and gin rummy, the grandkids were finally in their rooms. Exhausted Sam settled in the den in his comfortable leather recliner, which the children labeled "Grampa's chair." He picked up the newspaper and glanced at the headlines. Putting it down, he dialed Jeanne's number, only to hear her voice mail message, "You have reached Jeanne. I cannot get to the phone. Please leave a message." He looked at his watch and thought 9:30 where could she be? She doesn't know anyone here.

As Sam watched a rerun of Law and Order, his mind wandered, *where could she have gone and with whom. We don't talk much anymore. She's always talking to Sara. I'm beginning to feel left out. He dialed her number again.* Still *no* answer! "It's 10:15," he said aloud to his watch.

*

By the next night, Sam still hadn't heard from Jeanne. After the kids were in bed, he spoke to Sara and Bob. "I haven't spoken to Mom in days. Is she O.K.?"

"She's fine," Sara answered. "I guess between her job and school, she's busy and doesn't have time to come here."

"School," bellowed Sam. "What does she need school for? Is she becoming a brain surgeon?"

"Daddy, what a thing to say. You should be proud of her; to go to school at her age is great."

"She never needed school before, why now?"

"She told me she always wanted to go but never had the nerve. Her manager praised her on how fast she has learned the job. She explained how much the customers love her. They ask for her when they come in to shop. It gave her so much encouragement; she decided to give school a try. She's taking a management course. It might help her advance her career."

"Her, a manager? Now that's a laugh. She couldn't even manage a checkbook. I had to do it, as well as administer all the finances. What did she know about stocks, bonds, money? It all fell on me and now..."

Bob laughed. "The apple doesn't fall far from the tree."

"Wait! I resent the connotation. Are you insinuating I'm not capable of anything concerning my mind? Who runs this household?- You men!"

"Look baby, I didn't mean anything!"

"Too little... too late."

"What are you getting so excited about?" Sam asked. "Your mother knows her limitations..."

"Daddy, its the twenty-first century not the dark ages. You can't keep women in the kitchen with the babies. We have no limitations. No wonder she's so insecure." She shook her head and stood up. "I'm disappointed in your attitude. Now if you'll both excuse me, I'm going to bed."

"Boy, women can be touchy don't you think?" Bob whispered.

The two men grinned. The conversation changed to sports as the newscaster gave the nightly run down on the sports events. They dissected the management of the teams and the plays of the game. Bob, from Boston, was a Red Sox fan. Sam, from New York, rooted for the Yankees. The discussion and rivalry was endless. It kept them busy for hours.

*

"No wonder my mother thinks she can't do a good job." Not realizing she spoke out loud, she jumped at the sound of her own voice. She threw her shoes across the floor and thought, *I never saw my father in that light before. Has he always been so negative towards her? Bob tries to be macho but he has encouraged me into untried areas.*

As she hung up her pants and shirt, she grinned and remembered how scared she was when she became a member of the PTA board. *He brought me a new pen and binder so I would look the part.* While she washed her face, her thoughts changed. *But on the other hand, anytime I mentioned going to work, he said "He'd support me." Why bother? Stay home and watch the kids.* As she brushed her teeth she considered, are they the same? *Has Bob consciously kept me home? Have I kept me home?* Getting into bed, Sara made a mental note to call her mother in the morning to inquire about school and give her a pat on the back. She was reading *The First Wives Club* and chuckled, how they became independent, successful, and happy in their situation. How apropos!

-54-

Ramon walked past the Excelsior Boutique and glanced in the window. When he reached the corner, he abruptly turned around and ran back to the store. *The red scarf in the window is just Jeanne's style. She would love it, he thought, as he entered the shop.*

"May I help you, sir?" the salesgirl asked in a soft pleasant voice.

"I'd like to see the red scarf in the window."

"It's silk of the highest quality. Hermes," she said opening it to its fullest length. "The fringes add a certain flair..."

"Perfect. I'll take it. Would you please wrap it? It's a special gift."

"Can you help me miss?" asked a woman who had been looking at shoes.

"I'll be just a minute."

"I've been waiting, and I'm in a hurry. I have to get back to work."

She looked around the store for the other sales person. "I'll get someone to help you." Finding no one available, she spoke into the phone. "Jeanne, can you help this customer? She's been waiting for some time and I'm busy."

Jeanne came out of the back and approached the customer. "Good morning. Sorry to keep you waiting. What can I do to assist you?"

Ramon paled. He swung around hitting his hip on the counter. He saw her. She wore a fitted blue suit, which showed off her perfect figure. Her blonde hair curled around her face; somehow she looked younger. His breath was shallow and he barely got out, "Marguerite?"

Jeanne dropped the set of keys she held in her hand. Turning towards him the surprise written all over her face, eyes wide, mouth open. Her hands flew to her face.

"Ramon?"

They looked at each other for a moment. *My legs are shaking so much I can't move,* he thought.

"Excuse me. I can see the emotion of the moment. However, I'm in a hurry."

Being the consummate saleswoman, she shook her head as if to let out the cobwebs, Jeanne said, "I'm sorry. What do you need?"

"These Manolos , size 8."

Jeanne remained staring at Ramon. She did not move. After observing what just happened and sensing the tension, Amanda, the manager, came to the rescue. "Jeanne, visit with your friend. I'll help this lady with her shoes."

Jeanne nodded and walked towards Ramon. She hugged him and he held her tightly. He closed his eyes and inhaled her fragrance. She stepped back and separated herself. Her eyes focused on his. "When did you come? Why are you here? Is everything all right?"

Holding her at arm's length, he gave her his magnificent smile and looked directly into her face. He gained his composure. "I've been here a few days-- attended a medical conference. Most importantly, I've been looking for you."

"How did you find me?" she asked patting his arm.

"A coincidence -- or maybe fate?" He laughed, "I stopped here to buy you a red scarf. Now you must always wear it, this lucky piece of silk that has brought us together again."

She laughed, stood on her toes and kissed him full on the mouth.

Jeanne's boss told her to take the rest of the afternoon off. She just laughed and whispered, "After all you wouldn't be very good here anyway. The stars in your eyes won't be on the customers. Besides it's not too busy."

*

Jeanne and Ramon had a leisurely lunch in a small cafe. The acoustics were such that the noise level was contained. The soft chatter in the background made them very comfortable. The cream color table linens and matching dinnerware gave an elegant look. *I feel so good,* Jeanne thought, as she scanned the menu. Their meal; Caesar salad and filet of sole was complemented by a carafe of Chardonnay. Double Espressos rounded out the delightful repast. Lively conversation accompanied the meal.

"I never thought I would see you again," she said looking directly at Ramon. "You just disappeared."

"I needed to be alone. I'm sorry I didn't talk to you, But I thought you and Sam…"

"Never mind," she smiled, "You're here now."

Trying to lighten the conversation, Jeanne said, "How do you like the shop I work in? Pretty fancy stuff huh?"

"It fits you. You should always have the best." He reached over and stroked her hands.

"It's a great place to work. I love my job. I have customers who deal only with me," she bragged with a smile that lit up her face. "My manager says she doesn't know what she did without me. I'm an asset to the store. Imagine me an asset. How cool!"

"Why are you so shocked? I always knew you would excel at anything you undertook. You survived didn't you?"

Between sips of wine, Jeanne studied her glass, "Guess what? I also go to school. I'm taking a management course at the college. I go two nights a week and adore it. It feels so good knowing I can keep up with the other students."

"You need help in building your ego, sweetheart. You put yourself down much too much and too quickly."

Asking them if there was anything else they needed, as the waiter presented the check, gave them the message that the he wanted to clear the table.

As they left, Ramon looked at his watch and whistled, "Where did the afternoon go? We've been here almost three hours."

-55-

Holding hands they headed towards the hotel and the elevator that led them to Ramon's suite. Once in the privacy of the room, they fell into each other's arms and walked directly into the bedroom. A giggle escaped as she said, "I can't get over that a woman of my age would be having a matinee in a hotel room."

The gentle kisses led to more passionate ones. They undressed each other, giving no thought to reasoning, and fell onto the blue paisley printed coverlet with its matching shams and throw pillows. Slowly Ramon caressed Jeanne while he savored their tender kisses. There was no hurry. They were intent on making love, not giving into lust.

Ramon repeated, "Jeanne, Jeanne you are mine. I love you."

"I love you too."

When the coupling was over, and they relaxed under the coverlet, he propped himself up on his elbows, looked directly into her glowing blue eyes and asked her to marry him. "I need you. Please say yes and come with me to Venezuela. We'll be so happy together."

She turned away. "I can't answer you now. It wouldn't be right. Not after what we just experienced. My mind is clouded with the emotions of the day." She tried to focus on the present, but she drew back into time. *How different this is from other afternoons in a hotel room -- slam, bam, thank you Ma'am. How I was used by Marty, and, if I'm honest, how I used him to enhance my existence.* She shuddered at the memory and said, "I can't make any sense of it." As she stroked Ramon's hair she whispered, "Please understand." She kissed him deep and long. She was more passionate than before, so unlike herself, more abandoned. He didn't stop to think this might be the last time. *Not now. This was all that mattered.*

*

The afternoon light waned and the darkness of evening appeared at the window. The table lamp cast a soft glow through the room. They sat on the sofa, holding hands and basking in the moment. As they waited for the tea and sandwiches from room service, Jeanne decided it was time for her family to meet him. "Ramon, I'm going to make dinner tomorrow evening and ask the children to come meet you... By the way how long are you remaining here?"

"I have a flight home at the end of the week which still gives us a few days." A smile crossed his face. "Of course, should something important surface, I can always change my plans. In the meantime I would love to meet your family." Not wanting to cause any friction between Jeanne and her daughter, he cautiously told her that he had already met Sara. "Jeanne, I'm not here by accident. I was in touch with Jeff Atlas. Remember the P.I.? He gave me your New York phone number. The message gave me this area. I got your address from the internet and went to your daughter's house to find you..."

"You did? I never heard about it," she declared, raising her voice.

"I introduced myself and asked her to have you call me here at the hotel..."

She glared at him. "You did what?"
Look, don't be mad. I had to see you and this was the only way I could begin to locate you."

"I may look it, but I'm not angry at you. I'm kind of pleased, as it happens," her voice softened and became silky. She suddenly changed her tone. "I can't believe that Sara wouldn't tell me."

"Well maybe she didn't get a chance. Or maybe she forgot, what with the children and all..."

"No excuse. I'll deal with her myself."

Jeanne seethed as she poured the tea from the silver plate teapot and served the fancy quartered sandwiches perched so delicately on the platter. She continued rambling as they indulged in this wonderful light meal. "I'd like to get my hands on her." *What could she have been thinking?* Putting down the sandwich and picking up her cup, she said, "I wonder if Sam had anything to do with her decision? Do you think she discussed it with him?"

"Look, don't let your mind run away. I found you and that's all that counts. Forget it! You just reconnected with your daughter. Don't let anything ruin that or our evening."

-56-

In the morning Jeanne went home to shower and change her clothes and headed off to work. Once there she became involved in the store. A shipment of new clothes arrived, and she set out to inventory them, affix price tags, and display them in an attractive setting. Her mind was kept busy but every now and then a thought of Ramon crept into it.

"What are you smiling about?" Amanda asked several times during the morning.

"None of your business," she answered with a mischievous giggle.

Ramon called and asked her to lunch. "I'm really too busy to go out. I'll get a sandwich and eat here. By the way, I didn't get a chance to call the kids to invite them. I'll have to do that later and change the date for tomorrow or the next day."

"Great," he smiled. "That'll give us another evening alone. Make sure you bring clothes for the next day and plan to spend the night."

*

"Hey Ma," Sara exclaimed when she called her mother at the store.

Jeanne hesitated, not wanting to fly off the handle. "Hey yourself, kiddo!"

"How's your class coming? I'll bet you can manage Filenes by now."

Jeanne forced a laugh. "Sure, sure! Sara how about you and Bob and the children coming for dinner tomorrow? I'd like you to meet a friend." She hesitated a moment. "Although I understand you've already met him."

"Mom..."

The laughter turned to a deadly serious tone. "What were you thinking not telling me? What's wrong with you? I'm really disappointed. What was your motive?" Jeanne kept her voice low, not wanting anyone to hear her conversation.

"I'm sorry," Sara tried.

"You should be. I never did that to you no matter how much I didn't like your friends. I thought I taught you better."

Sara sobbed and could barely speak. "I'm..."

"Look, this is not the time or place for this discussion. I have to get back to work. Come tomorrow for dinner. I'll see you then."

As Sara hung up the phone, she started to question herself. *What did I accomplish? I guess it was to protect my father, but after last night does he deserve it? Though, he is my father.* As she left the house to pick up Brianna and Jeremy at the bus stop, she said to herself, *boy am I screwed up.*

*

That night while they ate, Sara informed everyone that tomorrow night dinner would be at grandma's. "We have to look and act our best. She wants us to meet her friend."

"A friend, where did she find her? At school I bet," Sam chirped in a falsetto voice.

Sara didn't answer and wondered if the invitation included her father. A wrong assumption! Too late now! *If I asked her, and she said no there would be hell to pay. I'll leave it alone and hope for the best. I'd better bring wine and lots of it. I have a feeling we're going to need it.*

-57-

Jeanne and Ramon spent the evening in his hotel room. In an attempt to make it romantic, he bought candles in the afternoon and an assortment of bright colored flowers for the table. Dom Perignon in a silver wine bucket with two crystal flutes and dinner was served by a waiter, which Ramon had arranged with the management. There was a Mozart CD playing softly in the background. The meal started off with oysters. Salad was the second course, followed by a filet mignon entree. This is to be a very special night, he thought. Maybe I'll get the answer I'm waiting for.

When the waiter took the dinner service away and they were alone sitting on the plush sofa sipping the rest of the champagne, he looked at Jeanne. "Did you think about what I asked you last night?"

"Ramon, I'm so sorry. I have to be honest and tell you that I didn't have time. I've been so busy, and you are such a distraction. You drifted in and out of my mind all day. I really need to be alone to think about your proposal. Please don't think that I don't love you. I do."

"Then what's the problem?"

She paused, put her glass down and turned towards him. "I don't know if I want to be tied down. I've had that already for more years than I care to remember... And besides I don't know if I want to live in Venezuela. Please, querida. I need time. Can I have it?"

"Do I have a choice? You make me putty in your hands. How can I say no to anything you want?"

Their love making that night was special. They melded together into one body and slept wrapped in each other's arms. It would be something they both would always remember.

-58-

The next day Jeanne asked Amanda for the afternoon off in order to prepare for the dinner. Her work ethic made her add, "I'll make it up." She had ordered a roast that morning, from the local market, and filled in with the rest of the supplies she needed. Living alone her pantry was void of special condiments.

Once home, she prepared the house, throwing any excess stuff into the closet. Everything must be perfect. She was glad that she had listened to Sara and bought the whole set of china, instead of the few pieces she originally wanted. The glasses were mismatched. She only had six of the same pattern, the rest were assorted. It'll have to do. This will teach me not to be so cheap and buy piece meal.

They should be here by seven, she thought. Everything was ready by six o'clock when she headed for the shower. Hair washed, make up perfectly applied, and her new lilac outfit, met with her approval as she looked in the mirror. *I guess I'll do for an old broad.* She smiled at her reflection. Her inspection was interrupted by a knock on the door. She checked her watch as she opened it. A grinning Ramon stood holding red roses. "I know I'm early, but I couldn't wait."

Jeanne arranged the roses in a crystal vase, and ushered him in with a smile and a kiss. "Sit! I'm all ready," she said pointing to the couch. He looked around her small living room and felt immediately at home. The warm colors of the couch, drapes, and rug made him feel comfortable. "Jeanne, the blues and greens compliment your eyes. You did a great job with the decorating."

"You didn't see the bedroom," she said with a flirtatious smile and a wave of her hand. "This is not the time. Maybe later! We'll see." She pushed back a lock of his black wavy hair.

The moment was broken by the ring of the doorbell. Jeanne pulled the door open pleased to see her guests. She gasped when she saw Sam. *What the hell is he doing here? I'll kill Sara.* Wondering how she could pull this off, she took a deep breath and welcomed the family to her home. She kissed

Bob and glared at Sara as she kissed her too. She needed time to compose herself, and gave an added long hug to the children. Sam bent to kiss her and she turned her cheek. He grazed her face.

Jeanne held each grandchild by the hand and took them into the living room. "I would like you all to meet my friend, Ramon. Ramon, my family! You already know Sara and Sam..."

Ramon smiled and extended his hand as he walked towards them. "Sara, nice to see you again." He approached Sam, ignored the scowl on his face, and said, "Sam." He attempted to shake his hand, but Sam didn't respond. Sam's brown eyes were cold. His frown caused his brow to wrinkle. His back straightened in a defiant pose. This is her friend? What the hell is he doing here?

"This is my delicious son-in-law Bob, and these two sweethearts are Brianna and Jeremy." The smile on her face could be heard in her voice.

"I'm so happy to be in your company. I've heard such nice things about you." He shook hands with the children. "Your grandmother is in love with you, and I can see why. She talks about you all the time."

Brianna smiled and blushed; her cheeks a pale pink. Jeremy spoke up in that little boy manner, "I'm in love with her too." Everyone laughed except Sam. He stood silent, scowling.

Jeanne saw the anger written all over Sam. "Drinks anyone? Ramon brought some nice wines and grape juice, for you know who." She winked as she poured the wine and juice in wine glasses. "Sorry they're plastic. I never got around to buying real ones."

"None of this cheap wine for me," Sam bluntly said. "Don't you have anything stronger?" and glared intensely at Ramon, thinking, *I dare him to answer me. I swear I'll pop him.*

Trying very hard to keep his hot Spanish temper in control, Ramon clenched his fists and considered *I'd like to get that arrogant bastard outside. I'd show him who buys cheap wine.*

"Sorry unless you want a beer," Jeanne answered. Pulling open the refrigerator, she grumbled, "He's lucky I don't hit him with this bottle."

The air was heavy with tension. Jeanne tried her hand at mundane conversation as she passed around the canapés; pigs in the blanket for the children and warm brie and goat cheese with crackers for the others. The little ones immediately loaded their plates with the hot dogs.

"Ramon, what do you do for a living?" Bob asked as he smeared the goat cheese on a Ritz.

"I'm a doctor of general medicine."

"And from your accent I take it you're from a Spanish country."

"Venezuela."

Jeanne smiled at Ramon handing him the platter of cheese. "He was my doctor while I was there. He's now a very good friend as well. He gave me my life back by suggesting I go for hypnosis."

"Big deal," Sam shot back, helping himself to another beer. "Can't we talk about anything else but your very good friend?"

Sara's face reddened and she felt the discomfort her father caused. She was embarrassed for her mother and tried to diffuse the situation. "Mom, is dinner ready? I'm starved." She assumed the hostess duties, while her mother tended to the meal in the kitchen. She took her father under the arm and diplomatically directed him away from Ramon. "Dad, sit next to me."

"Ramon, sit here next to the children." Sara pointed to an empty chair. They know a few words in Spanish. They learned from my neighbor who's from Mexico. Maybe they can practice with you."

As Jeanne served the salad, she squeezed Sara's shoulder in gratitude.

"Got any more beer?" Sam asked. He wasn't really a drinker, and after the third bottle his speech slurred. Mixed with his anger over seeing Ramon, the fourth bottle drove him over the edge. "Look here Herr Doctor, when the hell are you going back to your precious country? We don't need the likes of you here. We did just fine without ..."

"Sam," Jeanne gasped. "What's wrong with you? She looked at him. His anger tightened and reddened his face. *He's so bitter,* she thought. *As though he'd bitten into a lemon! There's something cruelly insensitive in him,* she realized. *Is this his true self? She remembered his outburst when she confessed her affair, and how humiliated he made her feel. I deserved it then, I guess. But now?*

He always appeared to be so pleasant, so quiet. But then again, when did I give him reason to act out? I never crossed him. I was such a goody -goody. Sam liked the movies, so I went to the movies. Sam wanted to go to the beach, so I went to the beach. He never asked me where I would like to go or what I wanted to do. Boy was I a sap. Passive little me!

Sam's whiny voice interrupted her reflections. "What's wrong with me? Nothing that couldn't be fixed if he would leave," he mumbled in an inebriated manner, as he jumped up and pointed his finger at Ramon. The sudden movement knocked the chair over and he stumbled, losing his balance. Bob bolted and grabbed Sam before he could fall.

"Dad, how about lying down for a while?"

Sam's face was beet red. "What, and leave her with him?" Spittle formed at the corners of his mouth. "Miss all the fun? The slut sure knows how to be with other men. No dice." He swung his hands towards Ramon, as he tried to grab him across the table. Sam's alcohol breath nearly smothered Bob and caused him to back away. But he was able to hold Sam tightly. Tears of frustration formed and he pushed Bob away, knocking the beer bottle to the floor.

Frightened at the outburst, Brianna and Jeremy started to cry. They ran to their mother. "Why is Grandpa crying?" Brianna asked, burying her head in Sara's lap.

"He doesn't feel well, that's all. Don't be scared. Daddy will fix him up." She barely got the words out. Her body tensed with mixed emotions, angry at her father. But in her usual passive manner, she immediately rationalized her involvement. *Isn't it my fault bringing him to this situation? I knew Ramon would be here, but I didn't think he would act like this. In all my years, I never saw this side of him before. Saying those things about my mother!* These momentary thoughts revolved through her head as she caressed and comforted her children, holding them close to her.

"Leave me alone!" Sam yelled, arms flapping. The crying jag made him weak as putty, which enabled Bob to subdue him and lead him into the bedroom and into bed. He was snoring in a matter of minutes - the sleep of a person saturated with alcohol.

"My dinner is ruined. Everything spoiled," Jeanne cried as she wiped up the beer. "I wanted this evening to be so special."

"Now, now," Ramon consoled. "He's just had too much to drink." His outside demeanor was calm, but inside a storm brewed. *How dare he act like such a son-of-a-bitch; saying such horrid things. How did she live with him all those years? He deserved to be thrown out of here when he uttered the first nasty word. I'd go into the bedroom and give him what for, except I have to act better than him. I wouldn't stoop to his level. But I'd like the opportunity to show him what a real man is.*

Jeanne plopped down on the chair, still holding the wet rag. "What's gotten into him? He never drinks." She trembled. "That awful accusation..." She remained sitting in the same position in a state of shock.

Sara sat quietly holding the children. Her anger abated, saddened by her father's outrageous behavior. *He's so jealous? Could the appearance of this Spanish guy cause him to act like that? I never saw him so angry. Even that time I stayed out all night. He yelled but not like this. Is there something deeper? Calling my mother such a name! Were there things in the past that I never knew?*

Bob came in and saw the depressed looking trio. He loved his mother-in-law and felt badly for her. He tried to lighten the atmosphere. "Mom, I heard you say your dinner was ruined. No way -- Dad'll sleep for a while." He smiled at her. "Give us some of your delicious food."

"I'll help," Ramon chimed in. Jeanne held the arms of the chair for support as she tried to get up. He took her hands and together they went into the kitchen.

Bob whispered, "What the hell just happened? Your parents -- the ultimate couple."

"Beats me," Sara answered as she guided the children back into their chairs. She kissed him. "You were great. Thanks."

The aroma permeated the air as the food was served. Their appetites quickly returned. Even with the delay, the roast beef was perfection. The accompanying roasted potatoes complimented the meat and the sautéed green beans topped with fried onions was the perfect vegetable. The adults had refills of the merlot which helped them mellow. Jeanne however, picked at her food. She twirled the fork through the edibles she so carefully prepared. She put her fork down and wiped her mouth, with her napkin, as if she had really eaten. A sigh escaped from deep within as she emptied her wine glass and put it down. *I have many decisions to make* she thought. *It's time I became an adult.*

The room was enveloped in silence. The only sound was the silverware as it scraped the plates. Suddenly the quiet was shattered.

"I don't want potatoes or green stuff," Jeremy whined.

"Eat them," Sara said through clenched teeth.

Starting to cry, he said "no," and pushed his plate away.

Sara got up and shook him. "Eat."

"Don't let it out on him," Bob said. "Look little man, take a piece of bread and watch the T.V." Both children scampered.

"Let's not let emotion run away with us," Bob articulated.

Dammit, Sara thought, *he's always in control and hardly loses it.*

"Let's clear the air calmly," he continued.

Not knowing quite how to act, Ramon sat quietly holding his tongue.

The stranger among them; voiceless, speechless, but seething internally.

Bob went on, "Jeanne, we're sorry we brought Sam along, but we really didn't know how to handle his not coming. Never thought it would result in this. I've never seen this side of him."

"It's not all his fault," Sara defended her father. "He was put in an awkward position." Looking at her mother, "I'm sure he never dreamed your friend was male. Most women have female friends." The sarcasm dripped from her mouth. "Husbands have male friends."

"Why don't we leave it alone? "Ramon asked. "Enough is enough. We'll never be able to sort it out. Your mother has had her share of aggravation for tonight. I guess I'll take the blame."

"No, no, no," Jeanne threw her hands up. "You're not to blame. He is and I am. I've been avoiding the future long enough. It's my responsibility to clear things. When he sobers up and has had some time to think, I'll talk to him and we can start to sort our lives out. In the meantime, maybe we can finish our dinner. I've had enough wine and am in desperate need of a caffeine fix."

As they were having coffee and apple pie a la mode, a disheveled barefoot Sam came out of the bedroom. His wrinkled shirt tail hung out of his pants. He rubbed his face and ran his hand through his hair. A bewildered look passed through his eyes as he stared at the gathering at the table. Coffee cups in mid-air -- food in their mouths -- chewing suspended. They stared back as if a ghost had appeared.

An embarrassed look crossed his face and he tried to manage a sheepish grin. He didn't talk for a minute as he gathered his wits as to why he had been in bed in a darkened room in her apartment. His throat was parched and his words could barely be heard. "I'm not sure exactly why I was in the bed. The pounding in my head gives me some indication. I guess I had one too many beers."

The children were the first ones up. "Grandpa, are you better?" they cried as they ran to him and hugged his legs.

"Sure," Sam mumbled. "I need to go to the bathroom to wash. Go back to Mommy now."

"I think you should go," Jeanne said quietly to no one in particular. She put her cup down gently and shuddered as she remembered the outburst. *I've lived with that man for so many years and never really knew him. Is this a dark side that I saw and automatically never admitted?*

Her thoughts were interrupted. "Mom! Hello, where are you?" I said you're right I'll get the kids ready and we'll go. Did you hear me?"

"Sorry. I was lost for a moment."

Sam sauntered out of the bathroom and went directly towards the living room. His stance had changed and he stood in a defiant pose. "I remember now where I left off..."

"Daddy, please let's go," Sara begged, holding his jacket. She tried to intercept and lead him to the door. "We've had more than enough tonight. Besides it's late and the kids have to go to bed."

"Sam, I think you'd better go with Sara," Jeanne said in a controlled voice, as she joined them and walked towards the front door, her sharp blue eyes fixed on Sam.

He grabbed his jacket and pulled the doorknob with such force that it almost dislodged from its hinge. "Go to hell," he yelled as he stormed out and left the others to say their good-nights.

-59-

Ramon helped Jeanne clear the table and started to load the dishwasher. "Leave it," she simply said. "Go home. I'm spent. I desperately need to be alone."

"Please let me stay and comfort you. We'll clean up and then we'll talk."

She flung the plate that she held. It shattered across the floor. Crying she repeated, "Not tonight. I mean it. I really need to be alone. My life has become everyone else's. It's time it became my own."

Ramon took her in his arms. "You need a good strong shoulder to cry on. I'm here for you." His shirt was wet with her tears. He took her face in his hands and kissed the wetness away. She grabbed him for support and he led her to the sofa. The lone light on the end table cast a soft glow to the room.

The soft kisses soon became filled with passion. He set her gently on the couch. She sunk into the soft pillows, still hanging on to his neck. Their lips never parted. Her need for him was apparent. She tore her blouse open and lifted his shirt from his trousers. As their bare torsos touched each other they shuddered as if struck by an electric current. Jeanne looked at Ramon's dear face as he entered her. They swayed in unison as if on a wave in the ocean -- the sounds of the water in their ears obliterated all thoughts.

Afterwards, as they lay huddled together underneath the multi-colored afghan that Jeanne had crocheted, he held her tight. He succumbed to a comfortable nap, her head on his chest. His last thought before he slept was *I guess I got my answer. We will be together.*

*

Jeanne silently crept off of the couch, put on her pink chenille robe, and went to the kitchen. The dishes, pots and pans needed to be done and put away. Her hands worked automatically at the task at hand. The table, devoid of all implements, cried for attention. She wiped it down with a cleanser and then polished it with a cream. She put the centerpiece in its proper place and surveyed the results. It met with her approval.

She sat down in the club chair with the last drops of wine left from dinner. I have to be straight forward with Sam. Yes, he has to know what I feel. I'll have to meet him tomorrow and clear the air. She was deep in thought when Ramon kissed her neck.

"Hi," he whispered. When she turned to face him, her face shone with the look of a satisfied woman. "You're wonderful," he crooned.

"Can I get you some coffee?" Jeanne asked. "I know how you like your coffee."

"Sure, why not?"

As they sat at the table drinking the hot steaming brew, Jeanne looked into Ramon's eyes. "I've been doing some thinking while you slept so peacefully. I've made a few decisions. But I can't talk about them tonight. I have to sleep on them. Words once said can't be taken back. If I feel the same in the morning, I'll have something difficult to do about it."

His expression remained pleasant. "I guess that means that you'll be meeting with Sam tomorrow. After tonight's demonstration, I suggest you meet in a public place. The man's dangerous."

"No he's not. He's confused." *His life fell apart during this last year, she thought, and he can't handle it. If the roles were reversed, could you?*

"I don't mean to be argumentative," she continued without giving him a chance to answer. "It's just that I feel so sorry for him. We have a history together. That can't be erased."

"I don't want your past. I want your future."

"Ramon... I think you should go back to the hotel. I'm tired, a nice tired, but tired enough to sleep for a week."

Not wanting to crowd her, he bade her good-night with a friendly peck on the lips and left.

-60-

When the first light crept through the window, Jeanne was surprised she had slept so soundly. She got up and did her usual morning routine; a few stretches, a hot shower, and coffee. She sat at the table, sipped the welcome drink, and reviewed last night's actions. She rehearsed her speech with Sam. Satisfied, she washed the cup, and made the call.

"Good morning glory," Jeanne said in a bright voice as Sara answered.

"Mom, so glad you called. I was almost afraid to…"

"I'm good. I need to talk to your father."

"Are you sure…?"

"Sara, don't make mountains out of molehills. I'm a big girl now." *Finally* she thought.

"Hello," a sullen Sam answered.

"Sam, I really need to talk to you today," she blurted. "Preferably this morning!" *I can't lose my nerve,* she thought, waiting for his answer. "Maybe we can meet for breakfast?"

There was silence at the other end. "Look Jeanne, I'm sorry about last night…"

"It's O.K. We'll talk later. How about 10 o'clock at the coffee shop on Sara's corner?"

Taking a deep breath, he hesitated thinking *she's probably going to let me have it. But I'll smooth it, I always did.* "Sure. Sure. It's all right."

As he dressed, he planned how he would handle her. *I'll agree with her for a while, apologize profusely, and tell her it'll never happen again, and so on. Finally I'll remind her I'm the head of the family and she should come home. Enough is enough.*

Tying his tie, he decided that he would not mention the creep. *He would ignore that side of her life. I'll concentrate on her giving up the notion of a career and school. Home is her place. We were happy there for so many years, we should continue where we left off; before that horrible accident.*

*

"Oh shit," escaped from Jeanne's mouth. "My test!" *In all the excitement I forgot to study last night,* she thought as she prepared her books and notes. It had been years since she had attended school, and she initially found it difficult to absorb the material. She had to study at great length and poured over her schoolbooks.

The management course she was taking covered information that was new to her. She loved exploring the different management styles. An active student who participated in class discussions, she surprised herself at the information she had gleaned and was able to share with her classmates. Her opinions were valued by her peers. There was an innate knowledge of managerial behavior that she seemed to possess. The discussions were very natural to her.

Her confidence soared with each class. The marks reflected her hard work. She made new friends and started to develop a social life outside of the family.

I'm glad I acquired a study style and a discipline that made me learn with an improved ease. It's so late now, almost time to meet him. Better get with it. Yet, I have a few more pages to read. Her studying was interrupted by the telephone. Annoyed, she picked it up. *This damn phone! Always catches me in the middle of something.* "Hello."

"Hi Jeanne. It's Barry from the class."

"Oh Barry. Sorry for the abrupt tone. I was reading our assignment."

"I hope I didn't make you lose your thought. I won't keep you. I know how serious you are--wish I could catch some enthusiasm--just wanted to know if you would like to join me Saturday night. My friend's art work is being exhibited at the Dell Gallery. There's going to be a champagne reception."

She felt her face flush and was glad he couldn't see it. She hesitated a moment catching her breath. *Is he asking me for a date?*

"Not hearing an immediate response, Barry said in a low voice, "I guess you're busy."

"No, no. I would love to go."

"Great. I'll see you tonight in class and again on Saturday. Eight all right?"

"Fine."

"I won't keep you. Now back to your studies. Have a good day."

"You too. Bye."

She remained standing. *Me -- a real date. Wow!* She sat down at the table, picked up a pen and twirled it. Thoughts of her new life filled her mind. *Barry's cute-- tall with those intense dark brown eyes, gray hair and serious nature. Sexy too! Best of all, he admires my brain and how hard I work.*

She turned the page of her psychology book, but her thoughts were of her upcoming date. *What'll I wear? I need something special, after all a date. I'll take the new purple knit pants outfit from the store.* She chuckled. "Glad I tried it on when it came in."

"I can't believe it -- a date." she repeated in wonderment. *After last night what did I get myself into? But I already said yes. Oh well, I haven't had a date in years. I've gone out before. But with Ramon it was different. He was my doctor who became my friend. The rest evolved. There was never a phone call with a request for a Saturday night date.* "Stop," she ordered out loud. "You're not a teenager—just an old broad," she laughed.

Jeanne was disturbed by the insistent ringing. "Hello," she yelled.

"Jeanne, did I wake you?"

She looked at the clock. "Ramon, it's nine o'clock. I'm studying. I have no time for chit chat."

"I just wanted to hear your voice and see if you could play hooky today? We could spend the day together. Maybe a repeat of last night?"

"We don't have extra help today. I'm covering."

"Call in sick. The store will survive without you."

"I said no. I have responsibilities which I intend to carry out. You'll have to find other amusements."

"What's wrong?"

Just because I feel so anxious about Barry, don't let it out on him. Ashamed at her outburst she said, "I've been studying..."

"Maybe you should quit school. Come to Venezuela. I can support you. You wouldn't have to work. You can amuse yourself -- be a volunteer. Perhaps at the hospital..."

Why don't they leave me alone she thought? *Everyone wants to run my life. I can't have any time to myself. If it's not him, it's Sam. What pain in the asses they are.* "Ramon, you're treading in deep water. Enough! I have to get ready. I'll talk to you tomorrow. Bye."

"Tomorrow..."

Jeanne hung up before she heard the last word.

-61-

It was after ten when Jeanne left her apartment. The sun shone brightly, and she had to shield her eyes as she tried to hail a cab. It was only a few minutes walk to the coffee shop where she was to meet Sam, but since she was late a cab would be faster. *Of course when I need one there are none,* she thought, as she ran down the street. *I wanted to be there first, before him.*

She arrived breathless. Her blonde hair was disheveled and a fine line of sweat appeared above her upper lip. "Sorry, I'm late. I had to study for a test and just got involved."

Starting with an apology certainly puts me on the disadvantage she thought, as she took off her jacket.

"You wouldn't have to be so stressed if you didn't have this insane notion of school."

"Sam, don't start."

The waitress stood with her order book in hand. "I'll have a black coffee," Jeanne said.

"I'm good," Sam nodded to the waitress. He had already started on his bacon and eggs and continued eating.

"Sam, I don't know where to begin."

He put his fork down. With a sheepish grin, he said "Look, about last night..."

"You were a bastard. I'd have liked to kill you. But it's done. I'm over it. Forget it. Today's a new day and we have to talk." She sipped the hot coffee, stalling to renew her courage. "We've been together a lot of years -- good-- bad-- but I've changed. I'm no more the perfect little wife -- don't want to be..."

"Look, Jeanne. No matter what I still love you. If we go home, things will be different. No interference from outside sources. Just us, our friends, our life."

"No go -- I can't -- I need more --I need my own life."

"You'll have it. You can even go to school..."

"I can what?" She was furious. She looked at him as one looks at an unpleasant thing. "That's the point. You still don't get it-- never will." She gritted her teeth and bent towards him. "My past life is over. I'm a big girl now."

Sam paled at the emphatic tone. His mouth was dry, like it was filled with cotton. "Over! You don't mean it literally, do you?"

Jeanne became aware of the stares of the people at the next table. Shocked at how she spewed the words, she took a deep breath. *I sound like a fish wife.* She changed her position, sat back in her chair and took another sip of the brew. Her demeanor softened; her eyes closed for a moment, shoulders relaxed, fingers wrapped around the warm cup. The anger lifted. *Why should I deliberately hurt him? He's not even aware of our differences.* She looked at him with sympathy in her eyes, and a voice !oft as if she had spoken to a child. "I don't want to hurt you. You have to know I love you..."

He got up from his chair, hands on the table, and leaned towards her. "You love me?"

"Don't take it the wrong way. I love you, but I'm not in love with you. I hope you can understand."

"I don't want to understand. What are you talking about? Love is love. There's no difference between kinds of love."

The waitress interrupted. "Care for anything else?"

"A wife who cares," Sam yelled as the waitress retreated.

"Don't make a scene. It won't help. We each have to make our own way now."

Sam tried to make her feel guilty. "Don't you remember how good we were? Aruba, before the accident. The vacations at the lake. Laying under the trees -- music in our hearts -- a full moon--just you and me. And then Sara -- trumpets blowing -- how happy we were." His voice broke and a sob escaped.

She would not allow herself to fall into the trap and counter attacked. "Sure I remember. But do you remember? Jeanne where are you going? With whom? When will you be back? Where were you so long? What's for dinner? Where's my gray shirt? Me, me, me. It was all about you."

"I didn't mean anything -- I just wanted you home with me..."

On a roll, she continued without taking an extra breath. "And those many times -- I'm going out of town for a few days -- dinner charges for two--whispers on the phone -- receipts for gifts I didn't get."

The coffee shop started to fill. Lunch hour approached. The waitress placed the check on the table and cleared the dishes. Signs for them to vacate the space.

Sam sat silently playing with the wedding ring on his left ring finger. His face took on a grayish hue. He seemed to have aged in a short time.

Jeanne squirmed in her chair. She reached out to touch his hands. "Sam, I didn't mean it. It wasn't fair. That was old hat. A hundred years ago. And I wasn't so innocent myself. It's really nothing more than I need to grow. You don't..."

"Can't I learn?"

Tired of the same old banter, Jeanne needed to end this conversation. It was going nowhere. "Let's separate for a while and see what happens. Maybe it would be better if you went home? You had already started a new chapter when you thought I was dead. Continue it and see how it goes." Jeanne walked around the table, gently kissed him on the lips, turned and left the restaurant.

Tears streamed down her cheeks like a fine rain. Her hands in the pockets of her jacket, head down; she wandered the streets not aware of anything or anyone. *Why did I say those things? He brought out the worst in me. It wasn't always like that. Could I have lived in a comfortable cocoon? It couldn't have been.* She shook her head in disbelief. *What would have happened if the accident didn't occur?*

-62-

She found herself approaching the boutique and pushed open the door. Amanda looked up. "What's wrong? You look awful."

Jeanne just stood in one place, shoulders hunched like a forlorn waif stranded out in the cold.

"Come with me." Amanda guided her towards the back as she said to her customer, "Sorry, she's not feeling well. I'll be right back."

Amanda pushed Jeanne gently onto the worn lilac sofa they used as a lounge to rest between shoppers. She kissed Jeanne's cheek. "I'll return."

Jeanne's lips quivered. She hugged herself for comfort as she put her head on the pillow. She tried to relax in the familiarity of the small pink room. She loved the colors of the Kandinsky print on the wall in front of her. It somehow made her feel better.

The sound of light music, which played when the door was open, indicated the customer had left. As Amanda came in, Jeanne ran to her. The flood gates opened and the waterfall started. Amanda held her tightly, patted her back, and let her cry. They had become more than manager and worker; they had established a friendship. Amanda knew about Jeanne's past and present and the men in between. "Talk to me," she said as she wiped her friend's face.

"Sam looked sad and beaten. Whipped! What did I do to him?"

"What you set out to do. You knew it wouldn't be easy. We talked about it. It was your decision."

For a few minutes quiet pervaded. Amanda heated some water in the microwave and brewed chamomile tea. "Drink," she said. "My mother always said Chamomile soothes."

Jeanne held her cup between the palms of her hands and gained strength from the heat. Her voice was stronger. Streaks wove down her face and left waves through the pink blush on her cheeks. The tears abated. "But when it was real..."

"Did you do what was good for you?"

"I guess so. But..."

"No buts. Either go with him or don't. And your Latin lover? What about him?"

She snickered. "He wants me to quit school, go to Venezuela, and do meaningful nothings like volunteer or play. He said he can support me..."

"Does this sound familiar?"

They both laughed.

Amanda giggled. "From what you told me isn't that what you're running from?"

"I guess so. I'm so mixed up. Am I getting cold feet? When I got up this morning I knew what I had to do. But now I'm not so sure of myself. If Sam goes to New York and Ramon back home, will I manage? I've never been without a man to care for me. Even after the accident Ramon was there for me."

"Look sweetie, shit or get off the pot. Do you want to be independent or have someone care for you? The ball is in your court. Catch it or throw it."

A soft tune permeated the air. "Oh, oh a customer! Sorry old girl, relax. I'll be back."

Jeanne finished the tea and lay back on the couch. She closed her eyes and began to concentrate on her dilemma. In a few minutes the sounds of even breathing and light snoring could be heard. She had fallen asleep to dream the dreams that would haunt her.

-63-

Sam went back to Sara's house thoroughly dejected. Sara immediately saw something terrible had happened to her father. His shoulders were rounded and he held his head downward. He seemed to have shrunk.

"What's wrong? You look like you lost your best friend?"

He started to cry and wiped the tears away with his hand, ashamed to show such emotion in front of his child. "Your mother sent me away. She said I should go home to New York and continue my life without her."

"You must be kidding?"

"Would I kid about such a thing?" he yelled, as he walked into the family room. He headed for his chair and dropped into it with the weariness of a beaten man.

Sara followed. "What happened? Was it last night? Let her cool off. I'll call her to make things right. Mom never holds a grudge."

"Don't bother. This is between her and me." He removed the jacket and tie he wore to look especially nice since he assumed the meeting would be trouble about his behavior. He wanted to look good. "She wants to grow and told me I don't. Whatever that means?"

Sara held her breath and in a low inaudible voice, "Is she going with Don Juan?"

Sam looked at her. He put his head back and gazed at the ceiling without giving an answer. He closed his eyes and Sara thought he had fallen asleep. She started to walk out of the room when she heard, "Only if he wants to grow."

She started to laugh which made Sam angry. "It's not a joke to me. Maybe to you! You have a husband and children and a life in front of you. I have no wife and only a daughter who makes fun of me. Where did I go wrong?"

"I'm sorry," she said as she kissed him on the forehead. "I didn't mean to laugh only it sounded so funny, if he wants to grow. Think about it."

"I don't want to. Thank you very much."

Sam spoke but it seemed as if he was talking to himself. "Almost forty years. What happened? She says I'm not interested. Everything is me. And worst of all I don't let her go to school. When I said she could go, she blew up and said she doesn't need permission. What does she want from me?"

"Dad, calm down. I'll call her and see what happened." She couldn't stand to see her father suffer like this. *What's wrong with her, she thought. My mother never caused such trouble. Everything was always tranquil. I don't remember them ever fighting; maybe a blowout from time to time but nothing constant. Are these the same parents I lived with?*

She kissed him again, smoothed his hair and said, "I have to pick up the children at the Y. You relax; try to get some sleep. I'll be back soon." She grabbed her purse and car keys from the hall table and ran out of the house. *I have some time yet*, she thought, *but I have to get away from this house. What a thing for a daughter -- to be in the middle of two parents who are having a hard time. I feel like a ping pong ball.*

As she got into the car, she realized if this animosity continued, she would have to make a choice. She wouldn't be able to have both parents together at the same time. Birthdays! Thanksgiving! Christmas! She shifted the car into drive and sped away with the horrible thought who would she choose.

-64-

Ramon ate his breakfast, French toast, at the small table facing the window. He was so dejected he didn't feel like going out and had ordered room service. Ramon agonized over his conversation with Jeanne. *I can't believe the change in her he thought. Did I imagine last night? Did she put on an act? Why?* As he ate, he stared out of the window, onto the street, and watched the people go by. They all seemed to have a destination, a place to be. *I have to talk to her*, he decided.

He could not have a mess around him and placed the empty dishes in the hall outside of his room. He dressed in his usual casual attire; navy slacks, white shirt and a camel blazer, and rehearsed what he wanted to say during the taxi ride to Jeanne's store. *What's in my heart--my love for her-- I want us to always be together--how she'll love our new life--always in unison. I'll captivate her with my Spanish charm and straighten this out in a few minutes.* He settled back into the seat as the cab sped along, smiled and felt assured all would go well.

*

Jeanne was on her way to the stockroom to get an item for a customer she was working with, when she saw Ramon enter the store. "What are you doing here?" she whispered.

"I have to talk to you."

"Not now? I'm working. I'm the only one here and I'm busy."

"It's important."

"Miss, did you remember to get me these pants?" the customer asked as she absently examined the rack of ladies trousers.

"Certainly, just a minute." She turned back to Ramon and hissed, "You'll have to go. I'll call you later." She turned and went into the back to accommodate her customer.

Stunned at the dismissal, he remained standing with his hands on his hips in a defiant pose. *I'll wait,* he thought.

Jeanne selected the brown wool slacks, sizes six and eight, from the stock. Her body stiffened in anticipation as she waited to hear the sound of the music that would indicate the opening of the door, knowing he would be gone. As she exited the back of the store, her eyes met his. She ignored him and waited on her customer, finally completing the sale.

"Ramon, don't crowd me," she told him when they were alone.

"What happened? Why the cold shoulder?" He moved close to touch her.

She shrugged his hand away. "I feel like I'm being smothered. I need some space. I need time alone and nobody will let me." She felt like crying but was determined not to. *I've cried enough,* she thought.

"You act like I'm doing terrible things to you. I only want us to be together. I can't understand..."

"You see, that's the point." She took his hands in hers. "No one understands. Can't you give me some time to sort things out in my mind? My life has changed in the past year. I've changed. I was so close to death-- I've got a new chance..."

"At what?" He raised his voice and repeated, "A chance at what?"

"To be honest, I really don't know. I only know I have to take it."

"Then take it. I'm asking for us to be together. Your choice; I'm leaving the day after tomorrow. Call me if you want to. I've tried but I'm not a man to beg." He pivoted and exited the store, leaving Jeanne rooted to the floor.

She leaned against the counter for support to help her calm down. The sudden ring of the phone startled her. "Hello, uh, Excelsior Boutique. Good Afternoon." Her professional voice automatically took over.

"Mom?"

She recognized her daughter's voice and heard a trembling sound to it. "Sara? What's the matter?"

"What's going on between you and Dad?"

"Sara, please--I can't go into it now. It's too much for me--Now is not the time. I'll have to call you later when we can talk or better still we have to talk in person."

"Fine! When?"

"Can I call you after work? I can't think now. A customer just came in. I'll call you." Jeanne hung up without waiting for an answer. *I just lied to her. There's no customer. I'm really something else--making everyone around me miserable.* She sat down on the soft mauve divan in the corner of the shop, enveloped in a myriad of feelings. She had this desire to sleep but was afraid to. The dream that overtook her when she dozed in the back room an hour ago was still real to her. She cringed at the memory. While she slept she had visions of Sam and Ramon floating by as ghosts. They haunted her every move. They followed her. She couldn't escape.

-65-

"Hey, Jeanne," Barry said as they walked into their classroom, "Ready for tonight?"

"Hope so. I studied but I'm preoccupied..."

"Not the test. Your mind's always on school. Our coffee date."

"I'm so embarrassed. My mind runs a one way course when I'm here." She hesitated because in all the excitement she actually forgot. "Of course, I remember. Looking forward to it," she added.

The class finished early. Students were permitted to leave when they handed in their completed papers. Jeanne waited in the empty hall outside of classroom 101 for Barry. She said good night to each classmate as they exited the room. Finally he joined her.

"Wow, this test was hard," he said as they walked down the stairs. "You finished fast. I saw you leave. First one too! Outstanding."

Jeanne didn't respond. Flustered with the compliment, she rearranged her handbag and the books in her arms. She wanted to downplay that she was the first one done.

They sat ensconced on a comfortable soft sofa in the coffee house on the next block, that served as a hangout for college students. At night there was a smattering of older adults. Jeanne was excited to be part of the mix. Jazz music encircled them as they sipped their cappuccinos. Barry told her how impressed he was with her intellect. "You eat up the information. I see your face light up as you listen to the professor. And your grades! Boy, I wish I was so motivated. I'm really not much of a student. I'm going to college to try to change careers. I'm a salesman at a clothing store chain and would like to get into the managerial side of the business."

"Barry, guess what?" she laughed. "We're related. I sell ladies wear and substitute for the manager when she's not available. That's why I'm taking this curriculum."

"I've no doubt you'll achieve your goal. Me, I'm not so sure."

Jeanne blushed. Her face felt hot and she stuttered as she answered, "I, I love it. It's my first experience with school since high school and I'm real excited."

As he finished his brownie, Barry looked at Jeanne and blurted, "You should go on to get a degree. You could go far."

"I never considered it -- so far ahead -- it's a thought though." There was a lull in the conversation and she felt herself drawn to the music. Relaxing in the moment she thought, *I never had anyone have such confidence in me. He has faith that I can succeed in something on my own. It feels good.*

Jeanne smiled, opened her eyes and sat straight up, "Let's make a deal. We'll be buddies. I'll encourage you and you'll do the same for me. We can form a study group - it's a first for me -- should be fun."

"Slow down. Let's take it one step at a time. With my job I'm not sure how much time I can devote to your project."

Several classmates joined them, with their coffees, and exchanged pleasantries. They teased Jeanne that since she was always first to complete her school work, if she touched them would it rub off. Laughter enclosed their space. They rehashed the test and a brisk discussion ensued. When they were all coffeed out and tired of the subject, they said their good-nights and each went their separate way.

"Barry, remember to call," Jeanne said. "The evening was nice," she yelled as he walked away. She smiled all the way home.

-66-

Sara and Jeanne met the next day. Jeanne had arranged to take a long lunch break. The restaurant was small, on the order of a comfortable English Tea Shoppe. The chairs were covered in a flowered print chintz with matching curtains. The flowing cloths and napkins complemented the decor. White and yellow daisies in small glass bottles sat in the center of each table.

I think I need some fortification for our conversation, Jeanne decided. "Sara, sweetie, let's have a glass of wine."

"Two zinfandels, and a chef salad," Jeanne ordered from the waitress.

"I'll have a western," Sara added.

"How's everything?" Jeanne questioned.

"Fine! Mom, come to the point. We never have lunch on a work day and I know we're going to talk about you and Dad. Do you want me to start?"

"Sure." Jeanne felt relieved since she didn't quite know where to begin. It was as if she had gotten a reprieve for a minute.

"What's going on with you two? Daddy looked as if he was hit with a Mack truck. He sat and cried the whole afternoon."

"Sara, I'm sorry that you got caught up in this. It's really not fair to you. I'm not sure you'll understand. You look on us like parents. We're more than that. We're people -- a man and a woman who happen to have shared the same house for many years." She stopped and took a sip of wine. She wanted to say what she felt, but realized it was her daughter she spoke to not a friend. *I can't tell her about all the lonely nights with Sam reading his mystery novels or studying his catalogues of office supplies. How she sat alone while he traveled always wondering whether he was also alone.*

The early years raising Sara had been different there had always been something fun to do as she watched her daughter grow. The sharing of new discoveries, PTA, Girl Scout Leader, party planner. But once that was outgrown Jeanne needed something else. *I'm not so innocent,* she thought, as she selected those parts of the salad that she liked. *Instead of standing up to Sam and insisting that I work or go to school or do something productive, I chose Marty.*

Wasn't that clever?

She shivered at her memories and weighed her words carefully. "I love your father, as I told him. But I'm not in love with him. My new situation allowed me to be on my own for the first time. And I liked it. Don't get me wrong, we had a good marriage with great times -- your father and I. But once I remembered who I was, the therapy allowed me to realize that I really was not happy with my old life."

"You always appeared happy. We were a family. You were always together with Dad, especially after I left."

"That is the point-- always together. You're a grown woman. Don't you want to do something for yourself? Do you always want to be Bob's wife, Brianna and Jeremy's mother, my daughter?"

Sara picked at her omelet and did not answer. She appeared to be in deep thought and Jeanne didn't interrupt. Suddenly, Sara blurted, "You hit a sore nerve, you know. When I told Bob and Dad that you were a store manager, Daddy asked, 'what did you know about managing? You couldn't manage the checkbook,' or something like that. Then Bob laughed and said, 'the apple doesn't fall far from the tree.' I was pissed, and if I allow myself to think about it, I still am."

"Well, you can understand. But don't wait your whole life to do something about it. Expand your horizons, make a niche for yourself. And that's what I'm trying to do now. I found out, it's never too late. Why, my classmates are impressed with me and my capabilities in school. How about that?"

The waiter brought their tea and pastries giving them each a few moments to ponder. Jeanne chimed right in, "Do it now! Don't wait."

"But, do you have to leave Dad? And how about Ramon?"

-67-

The sun peaked out from time to time and brightened the cloudy, dreary day. These variations reflected the mix of emotions that Sara felt as she drove home; glad and sad at the same time. The conversation she had with her mother made her realize that she wasn't a pawn between parents. They could both be hers, but under different circumstances. She felt the parting wasn't due to a particular hostility but rather to a conflict of ideology. Her mother would always behave correctly and affectionately to her father and her father would eventually calm down. *Mom is right. He has to go back home and resume his life. He needs a woman around him. I'll have to work on that*, she thought, and grinned. She would force herself to accept that fact, now that she understood her mother. It won't be easy. *I have a lot of growing up to do.*

Sara was relieved that her own feelings had started to emerge and didn't have to hide them anymore. As she listened to her mother struggle with her own frustrations of not doing anything for herself, she believed that she herself was not a second class citizen but a person in her own right. *I'm ready to become an adult. Wait'll I tell Bob my plans for the future.* A laugh formed as she realized she didn't have any plans yet. *Oh well, I'll tell him I plan to make a plan.*

Sara glided the car to a stop as she approached the intersection and a red light. For the moment she glanced around her and watched a very good looking, dark haired impeccably dressed man, cross the street. He reminded her of Ramon. *Now I have to accept the breakup of my family, but can I if she chooses to go with him?*

-68-

Jeanne had another sleepless night. Too many lately, she thought as she finished her third cup of coffee since dinner. She toyed with the People magazine and turned the pages scanning the articles. She moved from the kitchen table to the club chair in the living room and put on the TV for the second time that night. Her favorite channel, The Turner Classic Movie station, was already set. She had seen "They Died With Their Boots On," an old Errol Flynn flick earlier in the evening. Now she watched a Marx Brothers classic, "Duck Soup," and never cracked a smile. Usually she would have laughed until she cried.

Jeanne smacked the arms of the chair with a deliberate gesture and raised her body. "That's it. I've made my decision." As she settled back into the chair she said to herself, *I'll go to Ramon's room in the morning.* Relieved, she laid her head back, curled her feet under her, pulled the colorful afghan up and promptly fell asleep.

*

On the other side of the city, Ramon was awake most of the night. *Should I really go home now? Maybe I should postpone my trip? Will a few more days change the situation? Perhaps I blew up too hastily -- I have to curb my temper and my tongue.*

The constant ring of the telephone disturbed him from his dilemma.

"Ramon. You must come home. "Mama..."

"Lina, what are you saying? Mama-- what's wrong with her?"

"She had a heart attack. Oh, Ramon-- we need you..."

"Stop crying, catch your breath. I can't understand you. How is she now? ... Is she alive?"

Lina took a deep breath. "Yes, yes she's alive. I'm sorry to blurt out such bad news at once but we're very upset. You always protected us, mi hermano..."

"Enough. What is her condition? Who is her doctor?"

"She's stable but not out of danger yet. We have to wait and see. I called your friend Pablo Montez. I remembered he was a cardiologist. He's in charge..."

"I'll be on the first plane I can get a seat on. Tell Mama I'm coming. How is Papa taking all of this?"

"He's OK. He found her and called for an ambulance. You know he was always a strong man. But looking at him when I came into Emergency, I saw that he had aged considerably."

Ramon called Dr. Montez and was relieved to find out that the attack didn't appear to be life threatening. But at her age one had to be careful.

The first available seat on a plane to Caracas was scheduled to leave at ten o'clock in the morning. He booked a first class accommodation and started to pack. It didn't take him long.

I have to let Jeanne know I had to leave at once. He looked at his watch. It's Sunday, her only day to sleep, and too early to call. I'll wait until just before I have to leave. He closed his suitcase and called the desk to reserve a cab for eight o'clock. *That should give me plenty of time.*

Packed and waiting for the bellhop to carry his bags, Ramon dialed Jeanne. The phone rang and rang with no answer on the other end. *It's so early. Where could she be?* He hung up and dialed again and heard her message. "This is Jeanne. Sorry I missed your call. Leave a message and I'll get back to you. Have a nice day."

Ramon felt his temper escaping once again. She couldn't have gone to Sam? Or worse-- spent the night with someone else? There was a knock at the door and the bellman took his luggage.

"I'll meet you in the lobby sir."

The interruption calmed Ramon for the moment and he dialed once again.

"Jeanne I have to go home immediately. My mother is ill... I'll be in touch with you." He slammed down the receiver.

-69-

The taxi driver had to slow down as he entered the driveway of the Copley Plaza to wait for the cab in front of him to pull away. Jeanne paid the driver and walked into the lobby.

When there was no response to her knock on his door, she went to the front desk. "He checked out this morning," reported the receptionist. She couldn't believe it. Having received no message further completed the shock. *I didn't say no to him. But did my actions cause him to leave? He did say he was not a man to* beg. She left the hotel completely shattered.

The Boutique opened at noon on Sunday. Jeanne promised to work this day. The taxi ride to the store was mental torture. She blamed herself for his departure. *His leaving is one thing,* she rationalized, *but with no explanation.*

Amanda took one look at the blank expression on Jeanne's face when she walked through the door and knew immediately there was trouble in paradise. "What now? Your love life is killing me," she grinned.

"Amanda, he's gone."

"Ramon? Where did he go?"

"All I know is he checked out of the Copley -- no words for me." Jeanne sat down, her coat still on -- purse in hand. "What do I do now?" she wailed.

"Are you feeling sorry for yourself? Did you really want him? As I listened to you whine, I heard you wanted to be alone--independent. So?"

"But I needed to talk to him. Explain. Work something out..."

"On your terms? Look kiddo you can't have it all your way. By the way what is your way? You threw Sam out -- wanted Ramon when you wanted him-- growing up does not mean only yourself."

Amanda saw the tall blonde woman come into the boutique and start to browse. "Excuse me. May I have some help here? I'd like to find a sweater to match this skirt."

"Be right there," Amanda answered. "Jeanne! Go fix yourself up, you look a mess. Then get ready to work. That's why you're here."

The command made Jeanne jump up. She walked towards the back as if in a daze.

A loud, "Jeanne!" shook her out of her funk.

"OK, OK," she mumbled as she entered the staff area. The phone rang and as Jeanne picked it up she heard, "And don't dawdle." Her eyes lit up and a laugh escaped.

The afternoon passed. She had three big sales-- multiple pieces and all designer brands, DKNY, Armani, Versace. The commission would help with her tuition.

When the store closed, Amanda insisted that Jeanne join her for dinner at a small local Italian Trattoria. "Tonight you don't eat alone." The restaurant was quiet and only partially filled. They both shared a carafe of red merlot. The buzz produced the relaxation they needed. "Talk," Amanda said.

"You're a woman of few words," Jeanne replied. "But each sentence so forceful."

They munched on the warm bread in silence. "I'll wait," Amanda muttered as she buttered her bread.

"Hey--give a break."

"No breaks. You have to vent your feelings or at least tell me if you feel?"

"Of course I feel, only I'm not sure how. I want to be with Ramon-- but like Teyve in Fiddler on the Roof, 'on the other hand' I don't want any obligations. How can I do both?"

Their entrees arrived. Amanda started to eat her baked ziti but continued glancing at Jeanne, who only picked at the food. "Eat, honey. It's delicious. The warm food is comforting."

With the combination of good wine and her favorite lasagna, Jeanne started to relax. "I want to go to college. I love to learn --I don't want to be a salesgirl forever--I'd like your job..."

"Thanks a lot..."

"I didn't mean it that way -- manager of a boutique or a department in a large store -- but not where you are."

"Seriously, Jeanne my girl, is Venezuela looming -- calling you?"

Jeanne stared out of the window; heard the horns honk and watched the people walk by. They seemed to be rushing along in all directions. "Everyone is in such a hurry," she said and turned back towards Amanda.

"Why couldn't he wait to say good-bye? Why just leave?"

"Absence makes the heart grow fonder, as the saying goes. Will it?"

"I don't know. I feel cheated -- lost." Jeanne's eyes and the way she sat hunched over and played with the dessert, reflected the sadness she felt.

"Are you sad because he's gone or sad at being rejected?"

It looked as if Amanda hit a sore spot. Jeanne's demeanor changed. She sat straight up. "I guess I'll have to figure that one out." She stared at the plate in front of her. "You know, I never ate flan before I was in that Spanish country." Her voice softened -- "I did so enjoy Venezuela. I guess I could be happy there. I do love my Ramon."

"It's not always so good to be alone. I hate it. I love when I'm together with Mike. I'd jump at the chance to commit -- in a heartbeat," Amanda whispered smiling.

Jeanne hugged her friend as they left. "Thanks for being with me pal, and for leaving my colleague back in the business."

*

Jeanne saw the blinking light as she walked into her bedroom. She pushed the play button on the answering machine and felt her spirits rise as Ramon's voice filled the room. She played it back once more to make sure she heard it correctly and picked up the receiver. The long distance number was still recorded in her head -- it was dialed so often a few months ago. As she dialed and glanced at the clock in front of her, she realized the time difference and hung up.

*

Back in Caracas, Ramon sat by his mother's bed. He went directly from the airport to the hospital. The doctor in him reviewed the record, examined her himself, checked the tubes and machines and finally satisfied that she was stable, sat down and held her hand. "Mamacita, you frightened me," he whispered.

"Mi hijo, I'm getting better. Don't worry. It's not my time yet." Her eyelids blinked as she tried to keep them open. It didn't work. She breathed in regular rhythm.

Her hands fell loose from his. Ramon sat and stared at his mother, grateful that she had good color. The beeps from the machine were at a normal rate.

Jeanne must be ready for bed, he thought. *Maybe I should call her.* He turned towards the telephone, when the beeping cadence changed. He jumped from the chair as the nurse ran into the room. The even sound returned. After a brief examination, they realized that a change in position caused the disruption.

Relieved, he sat down and closed his eyes. He was exhausted from the time change and the anxiety over his mother. He was fast asleep in minutes.

-70-

Sam had his mail forwarded to Sara's house. Every few days a stack arrived. "Postman, Dad," Sara smiled as she handed her father his letters.

Sam was always a meticulous person, almost to the point of being compulsive. He made a big deal with the mail. It was arranged in three piles; junk, bills, personal. They were opened in that order. He used his trusty letter opener, glanced at the junk and saved it for recycling. He didn't have many bills, just the basics. Those piles aside, he opened one of the two personal letters. His friend George sent him an article about George Steinbrenner, owner of their favorite baseball team. He chuckled as he read.

Sam perused the next envelope. *Who the hell lives in Florida,* he thought, as he opened it.

Dear Sam,

> *Just a note to say hi. I'm finally settled in my apartment in Delray. It's very comfortable, light and airy. It has been a good change for me. I get to see my family often, but still miss my friends.*
>
> *I've been thinking about you lately. I've joined a group that goes to lectures at the art museum. Remember how we enjoyed them at the Met? What have you been up to? What are you doing with yourself?*
>
> *This area is a great place to vacation. Maybe you'd like to come for a visit? It would be fun.*

Keep in touch. (561 555-3214)

> *Molly*

He paused, and then reread the letter. Molly -- wow -- with all that happened with Jeanne I haven't thought about her.

"Dad, ready for some lunch?" As she put the food on the table, she asked, "Anything interesting in the mail?"

"George sent me a clipping about the Yankees. He and Ann are fine." Between bites of his sandwich washed down with hot coffee, he said, "I also received a letter from a friend that moved to Florida."

"How nice he thinks of you. Where does he live?"

Sam hesitated and concentrated on his tuna. He squirmed in the chair.

"He's a she -- her name is Molly. I met her at the Y and we became friends. We have many of the same interests."

She didn't look at him as she asked, "Is she the lady you spent the weekend with?"

"No, no. That was Sylvia. She was a little too pushy for me. Molly is just a good friend. His cheeks turned a soft pink as he mumbled, "She invited me to come to Florida..." His voice faded as he picked up the cup. "Sara, we've always been able to talk, but it's hard for me to speak to you about women. Please don't think that I run around -- I don't. I met these ladies when I thought your mother was..." He hesitated not able to say the word.

Sara offered no response. The rest of their lunch was in silence, except for the sound of the news anchor on the television. "There was a fire in downtown Boston, this morning, causing a massive traffic jam..."

As she cleaned the kitchen, Sara thought, *why not? Why shouldn't he go to see his friend? It sounds like my mother and father are splitsville anyway.* She banged the closet door as she put the coffee pot away. *I can rationalize but not be happy about it. Imagine an adult still needs her mommy and daddy together. What a joke.* Slam went the closet door again. "Damn," she yelled. "He can't even fix a lousy door."

Sam came into the kitchen. "What's wrong sweetheart?"

"Everything!" Sara walked into her father's arms. "Our world fell apart didn't it?"

He hugged her and confided, "Mine too." Sam whose voice belied their sadness tried to cheer his child up. He coaxed her away. "We'll be all right. Things will work themselves out. Mom..." He couldn't continue. The tears formed behind his eyes.

The roles reversed as Sara found herself comforting him. "Let's go shopping. That always cheers me up. You can buy me a present." They giggled as they got ready for the outing.

-71-

Jeanne arrived in class early as usual. The topic today concentrated on employee relations. She had read the chapters and was well prepared. A lively discussion ensued with participation from several students. Jeanne jumped in every chance she got. "The book indicates that a good work situation keeps the manager and colleagues from establishing a friendship just a good work relationship. I disagree. My manager and I have developed into very good friends. We still work well together. I respect her position and she mine."

Another classmate echoed the same position. The two hours lapsed and the students filed out of the room. "Coffee?" Barry asked Jeanne.

"Great. The other night was fun, as was the art gallery."

The coffee house was jammed with people who exited the school. They elbowed their way onto a comfortable love seat angled in the corner. "Jeanne, you were wonderful tonight. Your insight into the managerial arena is right on target. Even Mr. Marr seemed impressed. I can sure use some help with the work. Maybe we can form a study group as you suggested?"

A few other people from their class pulled chairs around them and a conversation unfolded. A study group was established. They would meet once a week, Thursday, for an hour in the evening after work. *With classes on Monday and Wednesday and this on Thursday, I'll be kept very busy,* Jeanne thought, breathing in the excitement around her.

Barry proclaimed, "Jeanne should be the leader of the group. She's the best one of us."

All agreed. She could not believe the status they elevated her to. "I'm flattered, but I'm certainly not the best one here..."

"Hey, Jeannie, don't put yourself down," Joe said. "Take some credit for the hard work you do. At the beginning of the semester you were like a scared rabbit, quiet and unassuming. But boy, have you blossomed -- you should go on to get a degree..."

The thought had been in the back of her mind and now she heard herself say, "I've been thinking about it..."

"Don't think-- you're a natural," Barry echoed.

Everyone laughed. *How lucky I am, she thought. I found my niche.*

"OK guys, you convinced me. As of next semester I will matriculate."

A round of applause emanated. The conversation turned personal and they soon heard about each other's family constellations. A friendship developed. They waved goodnight as they left the coffee house and as Jeanne walked away she thought, *they should hear my saga.*

-72-

Ramon's mother had taken a turn for the worse. He spent most of his time in the hospital, leaving only to change clothes. Lina lived nearby and he went there to shower, shave, and dress. He concentrated on making his mother well. The Gonzalez family gathered in her room, and they were permitted to remain. Certain privileges were bestowed to Ramon since he was on staff.

Ramon was a respected internist, with a specialty in hematology. He was called upon to consult on difficult cases that involved anything to do with the blood.

A young man involved in an automobile accident was badly injured. He had lost a great deal of blood and his life hung on a thread.

An elderly woman suffered two strokes in the same day. Another doctor consulted with Ramon about the most appropriate regime to dissolve the blood clots and prevent new ones from forming.

Between these predicaments, as well as his mother's, all thoughts of Jeanne left his mind. Circumstances had a way of changing one's behavior. His professional image took over and he became the doctor once again. The lover image took a back seat.

-73-

Sam called Jeanne. "We need to talk. I have to make some decisions.

"You're right. So do I."

They met in a local restaurant at five o'clock. It was early for dinner and the place was quiet. Sam requested a corner table for privacy. The lights were dim and the background music mellow. The room elicited a cozy feeling, but that didn't help either one. Tension was reflected in their body language. They sat on the edge of their chairs. Sam twisted his napkin, while Jeanne rearranged the silverware. The waiter took their drink orders and they perused the menu. Zinfandels warmed their bodies, but the strain remained.

Sam broke the silence. "Jeanne, what's to be with us? Are we still an us?"

Jeanne sipped the wine. She put the glass down and in a quiet voice said, "I don't think so. You mean a great deal to me. We're family. We have a wonderful history together -- years of good memories -- but I need to be on my own -- at least for a while. And I don't love you any longer. Not in the true sense of the word."

Sam hesitated, sadness reflected in his eyes. "I sensed that from the few times we talked. I just had to make sure. He looked directly at her face, the straight nose, the high cheek bones, the soft lips, her striking eyes, "You see, I still consider us a couple. I guess I'm wrong."

They played with the food in front of them. Jeanne tried to describe her feelings. "I need to pursue my own identity. I'm fifty-eight years old and have never accomplished anything..."

"Nothing? Our home -- our life -- Sara. Remember when she was born; soft, gorgeous yellow hair around that pretty face?"

She opened her mouth in protest. "I don't mean those things. I mean in terms of a career or even a job. I never... You know, Sam, I tried to explain why I have to dissolve my marriage commitment. But I don't think you'll ever understand. You need the comfort of love and marriage. I can't give you that you cling to the nest. You always go back to Sara..."

As they picked at their dinner Sam looked at Jeanne and thought, *when did this happen? Was she always so unhappy with me? Was our marriage so bad? I thought we were happy.* He stared at Jeanne, smiled, and said, "Remember when we first met? A softball game in Central Park! After the game, I asked you to join me and the team at a neighborhood sports bar."

She continued reaching back in her memory. "We watched the Yankees and had a few beers and burgers."

"You were an instant hit with my friends. That night we had dinner and when I took you home I knew you were the one. Our good-night kiss unveiled mutual feelings."

Sam smiled, shook the cobwebs from his mind and concentrated on the present.

"Jeanne, you know I care. Can we try again?" Sam tried to save his marriage." What if I let you do whatever it is you are looking for." I'm sorry I let work interfere with many of the things in our life. Looking back now I can see that what I once recognized as a virtue turned out to be a fault. There were too few vacations, weekends away, missed concerts -- things you enjoyed -- I refused to reschedule."

He pushed his plate to the side, as the past sped by in a series of disappointing memories. Jeanne's eyes were on him. She reached across the table and touched his hand.

"Sam, don't agonize. It wasn't all bad. We had good times. Yes, you worked a lot -- was away much of the time -- but you did provide for your family. Your priorities might have been screwed up,, but I have to take some blame. I could have tried harder -- when I mentioned going to work, you asked what could you do? Or when I wanted to go to school you said 'school was for children.' I could have asserted myself, but I didn't."

She took her hand away and wiped a few tears. The waiter refilled their water glasses and she slowly sipped the cold liquid letting the ice melt in her mouth.

Sam hesitated afraid to break the mood. He whispered, "It wasn't fair to you. I know you spent too many evenings and weekends alone. My travels always got in the way. I should have transferred to a local route, but I wanted to make more money. It seemed so important."

"Sam, it's not all your fault. I changed. The circumstances and the separation that I lived through -- I'm not the same woman I was before -- can't you see that? I'm so sorry. The years have gone by much too fast. It's time for me. I need to succeed for me. I can't do that with you. I don't mean to be hard hearted and unkind but let's not rehash this to death. It's done--over. We both have to get on. We'll always be friends but spouses, never."

The waiter broke the tension. "Will there be anything else?" he asked as he cleared the table.

Sam was speechless. He ran his hand through his hair as he stared at this strange woman across from him.

"Yes, thank you," Jeanne said. "We'll have the check." She stood up, placed her hands on her hips. "Please, let's part on good terms. Our history makes it necessary. Can we try?"

Sam sat motionless. His eyes cold and somber. "So no matter what I do won't matter?"

"I'm sorry," she said; kissed him on the forehead, turned and waived behind her, as she walked out into the darkness. *What a relief. I finally asserted myself and it feels good.* There was a bounce in her step, a new found lightness.

*

A week later Sam returned to his own home. He realized he had no recourse but to start over, alone.

Jeanne worked five days a week. She was off Sunday and Monday; Amanda on Tuesday and Wednesday. On Thursday when she came into the store, Amanda met her with a smile that lit up her whole face and announced, "Have I got news for you."

"What?" Jeanne asked as she took off her jacket.

"Remember I applied to Bloomie's for manager of the ladies designer departments? I went for three interviews and never heard from them..."

"Yeah, so..."

"I got it. I got it." She twirled around; hands raised in the victory sign.

Jeanne hugged her friend. "I'm so happy for you. You deserve it. You work so hard." Jeanne stood back, faced her, and asked, "We can still be friends, can't we?"

"Sure silly. By the way, you didn't ask who got my job?"

"Boy, I sure hope I can work with that person as well as we worked together -- but don't worry, whoever it is will never replace you."

"Shut up already. Sit." Amanda pushed Jeanne onto the chair. "It's you. You are the new manager."

Jeanne looked at her friend and shook her head. "Me? You must be kidding." She stood up. "I can't believe this. She pointed to herself and in a squeaky voice repeated "Me." Her mouth remained open, eyes wide in surprise. "I've got to sit down. My heart is racing, my knees buckling."

"And why not you? You're the best thing that happened to this store, except for me of course." Amanda laughed. Mrs. Kelly and I both agree, since she runs the other store, a reliable person is definitely needed here. You're it!"

"I still can't believe it." Jeanne's old fears surfaced and after she caught her breath asked, "Am I capable? I've only been here a few months."

"There's that old insecurity rearing its ugly head. You're as good as they come. Sales have increased twenty percent and staff morale is high. You have natural instincts and talent in all areas of retail. Dammit! Give yourself some credit. Don't you want the job?"

"Absolutely! I love the pace of the day. I love everything about the business. You know I never was exposed to this before. I was a house frau, a shopper, a volunteer. But now a manager! Wow!"

A customer interrupted their conversation and gave Jeanne time to calm down.

Mrs. Kelly, the owner of the store, called to talk to Jeanne about her promotion. They made an appointment to discuss salary, hours, and general tasks. Jeanne thanked her for this great opportunity. "Mrs. Kelly, you'll never guess the coincidence in the timing of this job offer. Last night I decided to matriculate towards a degree in business. And today -- I'm a real manager. How about that?"

-75-

Jeanne called Ramon several times and left multiple messages; asked how his mother was feeling and reminded him to call her. There was no response. *Guess he forgot me already. I have to put him out of my mind she decided. How could that happen so fast? When things don't go your way you just eliminate them from your mind? I know I didn't treat him well at the end and probably pushed him away, but still...*

*

Ramon sat by his mother's bed. Weeks went by and her condition deteriorated and was now precarious. Her heart had weakened to the point where it was touch and go. The severity required constant attention which Ramon assumed. He spent all of his time in her room; a cot was set up to accommodate him. The family gathered near Sra. Gonzalez most of the day. He hadn't heard any of Jeanne's messages, since he didn't go home. At this serious time he never thought to call her, convinced she didn't want him. He did, however, have fleeting thoughts of her. *How nice it would be if she were here to comfort me.*

The hospital's cardiac team consulted with Ramon and the treatment was readjusted many times. The fear that his mother would die used up all of his energy. During these days he divided his feelings between being a son and a doctor, as once he had between being a lover and a doctor. He had to put on a pleasant demeanor, as he felt responsible for the rest of the family. Being the oldest son, it was expected that he was the protector and would make things easier for them.

After two weeks of intensive cardiac care, Sra. Gonzalez passed on. Ramon had been very close to his mother and took her death hard. He entered into a period of depression, unable to eat or sleep. Some gray crept into the black shadow of an unshaven beard that darkened his face. Black rings appeared around his eyes and his clothes hung on his body. He stayed with his father and just roamed the house. He surrounded himself with photographs, stared at the television and generally did nothing, giving into a great fatigue.

One evening over dinner Lina scolded, "Ramon, you have to pull yourself together. She had a good life and you have to have one too." She wondered what had happened to him in the United States and his relationship with Jeanne. But she didn't ask. There had been no mention of Jeanne since he came home. Lina blurted, "How about we go to Paris for a few weeks; you and I? We'll do the sights and indulge in good food and drink. It'll give your body a chance to get back to itself. It'll also give us a chance to reacquaint. We haven't spoken of anything but Mama. You always told me I was a busy body and had to be involved with your life. So we'll talk. In the meantime we'll heal."

"I'm really not in the mood…" He squeezed her hands and his eyes reflected his gratitude for her interest.

She pulled two tickets from her pocket. "My treat to Air France," she said as she showed him the tickets. "Brother-- let's go." She put her hands together on her chest in a praying position. Lina whined. "Pulease."

He laughed for the first time in a few weeks. It felt good. "Sure, why not." They hugged.

Ramon notified his office of the impending vacation to France and returned home to pack. The blinking light of the answering machine caught his eye, but he didn't listen to it. Even though he consented to the trip, he was still consumed with his own sadness. *I'm not ready for the mundane outside world yet,* he thought, as he put his suitcase down. A musty smell emanated from the closed apartment and he opened the door.

A piece of paper fell to the floor as he unpacked. He picked it up and looked at it hard and long. Jeanne's face looked back at him. He crushed the picture to his heart. "I miss her," his voice cracked as he banged the suitcase shut. But she obviously doesn't want me. He opened the window to bring in fresh air. Sunlight flooded the room.

Ramon opened and slammed shut the drawers of his dresser, pulling clothes from them. Suits, trousers, and jackets were hung in a traveler. The rest went into his suitcase along with toiletries. He closed the window, took the case from the bed, and checked the room. A sigh escaped while he remembered their love making in this room and how compatible they were in all areas. "What happened to us?" he said as he deleted the messages, closed the apartment and left to meet Lina.

-76-

Jeanne was very busy with her new venture. Amanda and Mrs. Kelly taught her the managerial aspects of the job. She often stayed after the store closed reviewing computer programs for the inventory, payroll, and other business related items. She would assume her new responsibilities at the end of the month. Her plate was full. The class was concluding, and she was involved with finals and had enrolled as a business major for the next semester.

There was no time to commiserate about her personal life. Thoughts of Ramon filled her mind when the lights were turned off at night. The memory of their nights together pervaded her thoughts as her body relaxed in preparation for the time between wakefulness and sleep. She could feel his arms around her and their lips meeting as her brain drifted from reality to sleep.

*

In the morning as Jeanne opened the door to the boutique, a man wearing a black overcoat over his suit walked in behind her.

"Excuse me sir, we're not opened for business yet."

He shoved her in and pushed the door closed. "You are now honey. Hand over the cash bag and be quick about it."

"There is no cash bag. The store has been closed..."

He pulled a gun from his pocket and pointed it at her face. "Now - no excuses! There must be money here."

She shook with fear and opened a drawer under the counter.

"No tricks" he said. "See the gun."

Jeanne handed up a stack of bills. "Now empty your purse -- I'll take your rings too."

She did as she was told.

"Don't move," he said, waved the gun, opened the door and left.

Jeanne was cemented to the floor. She couldn't get her legs to work, nor her body to stop shaking. The sound of music triggered, indicating that someone had entered the store. She froze, panicked, and couldn't utter a word. *What could he want now?*

"Hey, good morning," a pleasant voice greeted her.

Michelle, the new salesperson, took Jeanne's arm. "Are you O.K."

Jeanne shuddered. "A gun! He had a gun..."

"Who? -- gun? -- No one's here. -- Jeanne calm down..."

"Call the police. 911..."

"What happened?" Michelle asked and ran to get a bottle of water.

Jeanne yelled hysterically, "Police. 911..."

"What should I tell them?" Michelle asked. Before Jeanne could answer Michelle handed her a bottle of water. "Drink this, and sit down."

Jeanne slowly got to herself. "We've been robbed. A man was here and pointed a gun at me."

"No way! Thank goodness you weren't hurt." Michelle placed the call.

Jeanne's fear turned to anger." We work so hard for our money -- how dare he -- and a gun." When the police arrived and started to question her, she shifted the anger to herself. "My fault. I was too tired to take the money to the bank."

They took the report. She described the man; white, about five foot ten, black hair, cleanly shaven, dressed in a blue business suit. She repeated how he held a small black gun to her. She quivered at the memory.

*

Jeanne considered not going to the end of the semester party at the coffee house. *I can't go she thought...my nerves are frazzled...my stomach queasy. I'd better go home. Today's trauma did me in.*

As she locked up, she changed her mind. *Who is that awful man to spoil my fun?* She headed for the school without realizing that this decision for her was an act of independence.

The coffee house was funky – low lights – sofas and soft chairs interspersed between the hard lollipop ones. Coffee cans were fastened to the walls amid posters for coffee products. They sat in a circle of chairs, drank their coffees, shared a variety of cakes, laughed, and generally had a fun time. Even their teacher, Mr. Marr surprised them and joined the group.

Laughing, Barry yelled to the waiter, "Give my friend Jeanne another latte -- the prize for the highest grade."

Everyone sang, "For she's A Jolly Good Fellow."

Lupe welcomed Jeanne into the business program. "I've been matriculated for a year now. It's not bad."

"Baloney; it's hard. You need a lot of study time. When she heard that the work was hard, Jeanne looked intimidated. She gave a half of a grin.

Barry came to the rescue. "Mike, It may be hard for you, but for Jeanne my dear, easy."

Jeanne was at home with her fellow students. They comforted her after she described the stressful situation she had with the robber and praised her ability to overcome her fear. A spring of affection permeated between them. Jeanne was glad she would now be part of this gregarious group.

*

Later that night, alone in the quiet, she reflected on the day's events. She realized what might have been this morning and how fragile life could be. What wonderful friends she had made, how they made her feel good, so wanted, so important. She had found her niche. *My world has become my paradise,* she thought as she curled up on the couch, wrapped in her favorite afghan and sipped a cup of chamomile tea. But a slight tear formed.

-77-

When Ramon returned from France, his spirits were better, lighter. He immersed himself in work. He involved himself in the most interesting and severe cases at the hospital. No matter how involved he became, thoughts of Jeanne drifted in and out of his mind.

Alone in the evening, he wandered about his home. He couldn't find a comfortable place. The memory of the fragrance of her perfume embraced him. He tried to concentrate on the mystery novel he had started on the airplane. "What does she want from me?" he mumbled as he closed the book in vain. *How can I help her? I respect her for what she is but, cannot see her for what she wants. I was raised that the man is responsible for his family.*

He finally acquiesced and placed a call to Jeanne and left a brief message. "Call me."

*

With the touch of the play button on the answering machine, Jeanne heard his voice. Her body gave an involuntary shiver; butterflies flew in the pit of her stomach. *What's wrong with me she thought? I'm acting like a teenager. It's just a call.* She reached for the telephone and realized it was the middle of the night in Venezuela. Setting the receiver down she sighed and said, "It'll have to wait 'til morning."

After so long, wonder what he wants, she thought, as she undressed and fell into bed. She was asleep in a matter of minutes, tired from the roller coaster of highs and lows that were reached this day.

It took a few days for her to return the call. She needed time to sort out her feelings.

"Buenos dias," Ramon's voice boomed over the wires.

"Ramon, it's me Jeanne..."

"Querida! How I've missed you. Your voice sounds glorious. Are you well?"

"Yes. And you? How is your mother?"

The silence on the other end revealed the answer. Still she needed to hear it.

"She passed on."

"I am so sorry to hear this. How are you coping?" She new how close they were.

"I'm better now, but I could use you here beside me for support. Forcing a vitality to his voice he said, "But enough about me." Soon in the excitement of hearing her voice, he started to babble. "What about you? How is your job? Are you coming here? You never gave me an answer."

"I can't -- I want to -- not now. My career is important." And with the next breath, she blurted out, "But so are you, only so much has happened to me. I became a manager and a full-time student. I finally have a sense of where I belong. I'm trying to be secure for my own survival..."

"And where exactly do I fit in?"

"I don't know. I need your love but I also need to understand my self-worth. I've been undervalued by men in my life and I need to be honest to myself. Can you understand?"

"Self worth -- I cannot understand. I never put you down. I know you are intelligent --sensitive -- strong. After all you survived a terrible ordeal. I don't live in the dark ages. Women in my country have careers and family.."

"I can do both but where? Will you live here?"

"My life is in Caracas-- my job --my family --my being."

Jeanne paused before she continued. Her mind became scattered. *I have to live my own life. I need to live in peace. What will I do in Caracas? I don't even know the language. My dreams--* "Ramon I don't know what to answer. I need time to sort things out. I do know, however, that I can't give up my new life -- I won't." In a much softer voice, she added, "I don't want to give you up either."

"I can only convince you, mi amor, in my arms and not with this damn telephone in my hand."

She heard the smile in his voice and forced herself to do the same. Afraid she would cry, Jeanne whispered, "Bye for now my love," and hung up.

Ramon kept the receiver to his ear. "Te Amo," he murmured to the dead connection.

-78-

Jeanne roamed the house like a tiger in a cage. She couldn't find a place for herself. On this Sunday, there wasn't even her job to break up the terrible loneliness. It was as if Sara knew her mother was in need of a friendly voice, when she called and invited her to dinner.

Jeanne hadn't spent much time with the family and missed them. Her whole spirit lightened as she walked through the door to the hugs of her grandchildren. After a wonderful dinner of veal scaloppini and pasta, she played cards with Jeremy and let him win every game. Later there was a tea party with Brianna, including some of the petit fours she had brought for dessert. When the children were in bed, she shared some quality time with Sara. Bob was at his weekly poker game. They sat at the kitchen table and drank hot chocolate. Jeanne reminded Sara, "It's like the old days -- remember we used to have hot chocolate when you came from school?"

Sara smiled at the thought, even though worried about her mother.

"Mom, you look awful, old and haggard. Your slacks are hanging. Are you sick?"

"I'm preoccupied - what with work, school, and my love life or lack of..."

"Um -- love life -- with whom? Met somebody nice?'

"Still Ramon! He wants me to join him in Venezuela."

"It's so far."

Jeanne continued without hesitation, as if talking to herself, while she stirred the chocolate. "I'll have to give up everything I strived for -- my new identity -- I'll become Mrs. Gonzalez, not Jeanne Golden -- I'll be back where I started."

Not knowing what to answer, Sara changed the subject. "Mom, you've taught me so much. I've started to become my own person in the last few months. I wanted to surprise you. I've enrolled in the university. I'm going to study art history and appreciation. I talked it over with Bob and made him understand I have to accomplish something for me. You know, I always was interested in art, the museums, sculpture. Now I can delve into the subject. I'm also planning to take a watercolor course. I used to love to draw."

"I'm so impressed," Jeanne said, with a smile "These Golden girls, like the television series. Is Bob all right with this?"

"Yes, since I got him to listen to me. You said assert yourself and I did."

"Kudos, my daughter! I'm so proud."

"Don't give up Mom. You've come so far... I was so hurt when you split with Dad, but I can now almost understand. He's so immersed in his own life and needs that he can't see yours. Thank goodness I reached Bob before he became too set in his ways. Thanks to you!"

-79-

As usual, Sam moped around his house and settled with the television in the family room. Pictures on the wall surrounded him with memories of Jeanne and their life together. How happy we look, he thought, as he stared at them. Yes, so many happy years; *so long ago. And now, nothing. I feel empty, drained.* "You look like a zombie," he said to his image in the mirror. Empty eyes, shoulders hunched, the dark shadow of an unshaven face looked back at him. "You look like hell."

He leaned back in the club chair and sucked in a deep breath. "I should care, but I don't," he said to the four walls.

*

One afternoon, after sitting in a chair for hours rehashing the last meeting with Jeanne, his emotions switched gears. Anger set in. He jumped up, ran to the bedroom, flung open her closet, He pulled the garments and threw them on the bed. *She wants a new life, then let her get new clothes.* He picked up the telephone and called the Salvation Army.

"I have a bunch of clothes. When can you pick them up?" Sam yelled.

As he hung up the phone, the rage abated. He felt weak and wobbly and needed a chair. Tears welled up and he sat with his head in his hands. "Why do I deserve this?" he asked himself. "How did it all go wrong?"

The sound of the doorbell shocked him from his depressed mood.

"Hey Sam, what took you so long? You got a girl in here or what?" George asked as he walked through the door.

"Very funny," Sam answered in a sarcastic tone.

"You look like shit. Get cleaned up. Morty's giving a talk on his new book. A mystery about senior citizen detectives. He needs our support.."

"I'm not in the mood..."

George got down on one knee. "Do you want me to beg? Stop feeling sorry for yourself, get your ass in a sling, and move it, buster. Ann is home with a cold, and I need a date."

He managed a quick laugh, in spite of himself. He showered, shaved, and dressed in a matter of minutes, suddenly feeling better.

*

As they entered the center, some of Sam's buddies welcomed him by shaking hands, and patting him on his back. "Where ya been? Haven't seen you in a dog's age. Glad to see ya pal."

He felt a soft tap on his shoulder and a feminine voice purred in his ear, "Sammy."

"Sylvia," he muttered finding himself in the midst of a hug. He stood straight with his arms at his sides, feeling a blush start to creep up his face.

"Relax and give Sylvia a real hug," she said with a laugh. She took his arms and wrapped them around her. "I missed you. I heard you were by your daughter. Glad to have you home."

Sam released himself as she patted his cheek and gave him a kiss on the lips. He felt the heat in his cheeks as catcalls and whistles came from behind.

Sylvia stood coquettishly, arms entwined with Sam's. She batted her eyes, set her face at an angle and pouted her lips. "Jealous?" she asked flirtatiously.

The president of the group called the meeting to order and introduced Morty Weisman. Morty spoke about his background, his vocation, and how he started his hobby as a writer.

"This was something I developed when I joined a creative writing class. The members of my class were my best critics and gave me the encouragement to go on. I thank them for all of their input in my novel and for the friendships that evolved."

A short synopsis of the book followed; *"A family disappeared with no notes or messages as to their whereabouts. There were bullet holes and blood scattered about. The police weren't able to find the missing persons. The missing man's father, a retired cop, called his friends together to help him find his children. These seniors thus became detectives and therein lay the plot."*

Sylvia sat next to Sam and held his hand. He didn't remove it. It feels good, he said to himself surprised at his reaction. *She looks wonderful he thought, sexy. The tight sweater and skirt, always in a bright color, accentuated her slim figure.* Sam bought Sylvia a book and after the signing, coffee and desserts were served. They renewed their friendship catching up on the news of the past few months. He told her about Jeanne's reappearance and her new quest for independence.

"I can't believe the change in her," he said as he sipped his drink. "She isn't the same woman I lived with all these years. College, a career..." He stopped short of telling her about Ramon.

"Look sweetie let her be. She obviously wants a different life. One that doesn't include you. You do the same." The lilt in her voice always made him feel good.

Sam smiled and remembered their weekend at the Cape and what fun they had. "Guess you're right. Say maybe we could..."

Suddenly Sylvia turned as she heard a familiar voice. "Honey," she said to the man who approached them. She met him with a kiss and took his arm. "Sam I would like you to meet my boyfriend. Joe, my friend Sammy."

Sam remained speechless. He shook Joe's hand by reflex. "Nice to meet you Sam," Joe's tone was anything but friendly.

"Ready to go Syl?-- the car's parked by the door. It's still early-- thought we might have a nightcap? I've got some good booze at my place."

"Swell baby. Good night Sammy. Keep in touch. I'll get you out of the doldrums."

Sam was flabbergasted. His hand still held the empty paper cup. George saw how shocked his friend looked and came over. "Get a grip," he admonished as he threw the cup away. In a gentle voice that had a bitter edge to it, he said, "How do you like that--holding on to you, kissing you. I wondered how long it would be before she told you about *her* beau. What a showoff he is. He struts around like he won the prize at the carnival. Some prize! I guess she needs a few guys. One's not enough for that tramp; one in bed and one on the hook."

Sam added, "Funny how an old broad can still be considered a tramp."

They both burst out laughing. "You always know how to joke and make me laugh," Sam snickered. "Thanks."

The two old friends left the center and as they got into George's car Sam revealed a secret. "You know she always intimidated me. I never really cared for her, not in the real sense, but she was so much fun. We did things I would never believe an old geezer would or could do. Of course, I had to endure that constant chatter..."

Again, laughter echoed in the air.

-80-

Jeanne and Ramon spoke on the phone regularly at least once a week; usually Sunday morning when there was no work. They discussed their jobs, her school, his patients and other mundane events.

"Jeanne" Ramon said, "I'm not happy with a transatlantic relationship connected by a wire. I need something real..."

"What's the alternative? You won't come here and I can't come there."

"We're at an impasse. Let's have some space. Distance -- no contact for three months and see what happens..."

"But..."

"You adjust to your new life style, and I will resume mine. Then we'll talk."

She frowned; her heart pounded. In an instant she tried to visualize life without him. Even though they were thousands of miles apart there was a comforting tie. She felt connected. "I'll miss you." Jeanne's voice betrayed her fears.

"Me too," he said determined not to falter. "But we have to give it a rest because if it isn't to be we have to be prepared."

Ramon didn't realize he had the strength to sever contact -- but he did.

Jeanne was devastated. She needed to keep their attachment going in the hopes that he might have a change of mind and come to her. She wanted it to be her way.

*

And so, life went on. Amanda came to the store to see the new inventory system Jeanne had instituted; a program to track the merchandise. It was easier and more efficient in all categories; items ordered, received, sold, in stock, reorder.

"What an outstanding program," Amanda gushed with pride for her friend's accomplishment.

Jeanne showed each nuance of the prototype. "This store and the

Excelsior II run much smoother since the inception of this internal control program. We have the capability of coordinating our stock with more proficiency. It works well."

Amanda smiled. "Your education is paying off, my dear. Say, would you let me bring this program to the administration of my store? We could sure use it. I'm sure I could get them to approve monetary compensation for you. You worked so hard you deserve it. Hey, you should patent it and sell it to other retail establishments. Your own business venture! A real entrepreneur!"

Jeanne was flabbergasted. "My own company-- I never thought..."

The two women talked as they walked to the restaurant for dinner. The streets were crowded with people-- their work day finished. The area once dilapidated and run down, was recently revitalized. Store fronts featured attractive displays. Upscale restaurants and bars were refined with understated sophistication. A pleasant cacophony of sound emanated from the masses. Jeanne floated with the thoughts of creating her own business.

"What have you heard from the Spaniard?" Amanda could see the change come over her friend. Jeanne's gait slowed. They had been walking arm in arm and Jeanne pulled her hand away.

"He... he wants no more contact between us," she blurted. "No more..."

"How come?"

"It's my fault -- I can't commit -- I won't commit." She stopped and turned to face Amanda, "I don't want marriage -- I think -- but I would like him in my life-- he wants all or nothing. That damn macho stubbornness."

"Too bad, toots," Amanda quipped looking at her friend. "You can't have both sides of the ocean, it's too big. You seem to be making your bed alone and you'll have to sleep in it -- alone."

Jeanne laughed. "A real friend you are, full of compassion."

"C'est la vie, ma cherie. You are burning your bridges so to speak, so stop whining. Let's have a gooey dessert instead."

Jeanne hugged her pal in gratitude for the warmth of their friendship.

-81-

Many changes took place during the next weeks. It seemed as if all of their lives were headed in different directions.

Ramon immersed himself in a new research project and spent long hours between the hospital lab and its voluminous library. When at last he got home he fell into bed. Sometimes he didn't even go home, he just curled up on a couch in the doctor's lounge. He didn't allow himself any time to think and when he did he realized how much he enjoyed his new endeavor. "I can't believe how much I like doing research," he told a colleague. *Out of an old sorrow, I found a new niche for myself,* he thought.

Jeanne listened to the advice given her; she had her computer program patented and started to investigate the different ways to market it. It was sold immediately to Amanda's department store. Amanda was rewarded for her find, with a promotion to manage the entire women's division. Jeanne received a hefty fee.

The two women were well on their way to becoming successful business contemporaries.

*

Sam called Molly and they began to speak several times a week. He told her about the center and Sylvia and her new boyfriend. "Same old Sylvia," he laughed. Still wants all the men around her like a queen bee."

They both had a good laugh although Molly still remembered the hurt she felt during the weekend she was alone while *they* were at the Cape.

Sam planned to visit Molly in the near future. "I have to get my life in order, before I make a real plan," he told her. "I'm still at loose ends. It's hard for me to be by myself. I liked being a couple. The house is quiet, I'm unsure of many things. I miss having someone next to me, to share..."

His voice faltered and he wondered how he could say these things -- reveal his feelings...

"I understand," she said in a soft, comforting voice.. "I know change is not easy especially at our age. It'll come."

He loved her compassion and caring. "You know, Mol, I could never talk so freely to anyone in my life. Not even to Jeanne in all the years..."

"Sam, maybe it's just timing, that's all. Don't beat yourself up. When you're ready, I'll be here."

-82-

"Mom, we came home late last night. Too late to call, "Sara told Jeanne as they spoke on the phone. "The visit with Dad was good..."

"How is he?" Jeanne asked as she washed her breakfast dishes.

"He looks well, a little thin perhaps, but well. He's renewed his poker night with the guys and his evenings at the Y..."

"I'm so glad. I've been feeling guilty about my actions. He's really a good man, honey, and probably didn't deserve the agita I gave him."

"I won't go into that," Sara said. "That's between you and Daddy. I love you both. I'm not taking sides."

"My, my how insightful you are, my dear child..."

"Ma, sarcasm isn't your usual style. I'll ignore it this time..."

Sara continued before Jeanne had a chance to apologize for her tone. "I have an early class, but have time for a quick lunch. How about it? I'll bring the things I brought from home for you."

"You bet. Today, at twelve at the usual?"

"See ya, and I'll bring the stuff."

*

Sara greeted her mother with a kiss and handed her a Shirley Temple doll.

"My doll, you remembered," Jeanne screamed and hugged her 'Shirley' and her daughter.

"Mom I also brought some family photos; especially of your parents. I left those that were displayed in frames for Dad and only took some from the albums. That's all there is. Dad gave your clothes away, I'm so sorry. He didn't want to be reminded of you."

Jeanne hugged Sara. "That's O.K. honey, I didn't have the strength to go back to the old house, so I'm very appreciative you remembered how much I love this doll. I always wanted to give her to you and I will, soon, but now I need this security. Foolish aren't I?" Jeanne held her daughter tightly for an unusually long time, almost afraid to let go.

"I'll wait," Sara whispered as she returned the embrace. And someday I'll pass it along to Brianna."

Holding her mother at bay Sara suggested, "Why don't you play dolls with Brianna? She would love it."

"Imagine my granddaughter will soon play with my doll. How fast the years evolve. It seems as if it was just a few days ago that I played with my mother." While thoughts of her own childhood whirled around her. Jeanne continued, "She was my playmate – she took the place of sisters or brothers. We played dolls, had tea parties, what fun! Shopping expeditions were in the finest stores; nothing ordinary for us. Sometimes I was a ballerina and my mother a famous Prima Dona." Jeanne closed her eyes and smiled, totally relaxed with her memories.

Sara sat quietly, not wanting to interrupt the reverie.

"Now that I think about it, we always were professional women; I, a lawyer, and Mom, a judge, or I was a doctor and Mom the head of the hospital. She constantly encouraged me to go to college, to always strive for a higher degree. "A woman has to be able to provide for herself --never depend on a man -- achieve all that you can and more."

The remembrances flooded Jeanne's head. "My mother never included herself in those dreams, as she chose to remain a housewife with no formal education. I wonder why? There was so much drive directed at me -- what about her?

"Mom, maybe she was satisfied with her life."

Jeanne surprised herself as she heard her own voice, "I promised I would always excel..."

*

Jeanne went home, spent from the flood of memories. After a while she dozed, with Shirley secure in her arms. In her subconscious she relived the day of her high school graduation -- valedictorian along with a scholarship to Columbia, an Ivy League university. How happy her parents had been, their smiles illuminated the night. Her mother had whispered as she embraced her, "You're on your way sweetheart, to achieve what I never did." Jeanne woke with a start, the dream so vivid she felt her mother's arms around her.

As she sat on the bed and took her shoes off, thoughts converged about the events that followed that happy time. Jeanne met Sam during their first year at college. He was two years ahead, enrolled in business administration. *How fast he could reckon numbers,* she recalled with a smile. It was love at first sight in Central Park. They moved in together off campus and started life as a couple. Jeanne begged Sam to keep this a secret from her parents, knowing full well how her mother would be, if she found out. "Nothing must get in the way of your studies and dreams," was a constant remark.

But in a matter of a few months their living arrangements had to be revealed. Jeanne was pregnant. They were both very happy about the baby and quietly eloped, promising to live together forever.

They were so excited and when they broke the news her father overjoyed with the prospect of the new arrival shared in their happiness. Jeanne could still feel the bitter taste in her mouth when she saw the expression on her mother's face.

"Pregnant! Married! How dare you -- our dreams -- my dreams -- disappoint..."

With outstretched arms, Jeanne stepped toward her mother. "Mom, I'll finish college, I swear. I'll be something special for you, I promise." Her mother recoiled as if bitten by an insect. Jeanne was devastated.

And that promise wasn't to be. Sam needed to devote time to complete his college education and start in with his career. With only a part time job he was barely able to support his family. Jeanne needed to bring some money into the household. She quit school, cared for the baby during the day, and waitressed in the local coffee shop in the evenings while Sam studied. When Sara was born, they made peace with her mother. Sara soon became the apple of her grandmother's eye. But she could hear her mother talk to Sara from time to time. "... college. Your mother never did..."

Jeanne sighed as she looked at the pictures of her parents. I don't think she ever forgave me for not making something of myself. I always had the feeling she thought, a housewife -- just a *housewife*.

Jeanne was too worked up to sleep and over a cup of tea, considered that maybe her mother was the force that had pushed her, these last months. *I always tried so hard to please her. Perhaps my promise still haunts me or rather gives me the impetus to end my old life and start anew. Maybe now I can justify the change in my behavior. I always needed a man in my life, or so I thought, but now -- do I? Maybe I can be happy alone and live for me and do what I want. At least I'll try.*

See, Mom, like you said...

As she put the silver frame back on the dresser, Jeanne contemplated her new life and the recent achievements. She straightened her back, put her hands on her hips, looked straight at the picture, with a smile on her face, and in a strong voice said, "Mama, I manage a fancy store, have a little business and will soon get my degree. I think I'm finally a success. Have I made you proud? After all, I promised you, didn't I?"

-83-

Jeanne and Amanda no longer had the luxury of meeting weekly for lunch. As each one climbed the ladder of success, there were fewer occasions for socializing and girl talk. However, they still found time for each other on the phone, and they even managed to squeeze in an occasional meal.

"Jeanne, my friend," Amanda laughed, as they kissed hello in the restaurant, "I didn't see you in so long I wondered if I would recognize you."

"Ha, ha. Always the joker. But you're right. It's been a long time. I do know that I never ever want to give up this friendship -- it means so much to me."

"No way, kiddo -- friends to the end for us, and lighten up. Don't be so serious all the time."

As they sipped their favorite zinfandels, Jeanne filled Amanda in on what has been happening. She sat on the edge of her chair, her voice raised with excitement, a silly grin on her face. "Amanda, guess what... I've been made a partner!"

Amanda put her wine glass down so hard a few drops splattered on the tablecloth forming a heart. "A partner; no way!"

"Yes ma'am, Mrs. Kelly gave me two percent." Jeanne was pleased at how the stunned look on her friend's face suddenly beamed. "We decided to open another store. I'm very involved in the planning and am going to be the district manager for this small chain. I'll also be buying for all the stores."

"What a feat -- buying too. But it shouldn't be that hard for you. After all the merchandise will be the same in all of the stores, no?"

"No. I suggested that the themes vary. One store will have affordable clothes, one upscale, another designer cocktail dresses and gowns. The boutique will take on a funkier look to include shoes, handbags, and the like."

"Wow. No wonder she made you a partner, a small one, but never-the-less... seriously, I'm thrilled for you." Amanda got up and hugged her friend. "I guess I made the right choice when I hired you." She laughed, "You even outdid me. Let's toast to your success."

"You know, you're no slouch yourself. Look how you've climbed the corporate ladder -- vice president in charge of merchandising. I think a toast is in order for both of us."

"By the way, so how's school?"

"Don't ask -- I'm swamped. It's the end of the semester and tests and papers are choking me. I don't even have any time to join my friends after class like I used to. No more fun. If I allow myself the luxury of meeting over coffee, my mind is on the work I have ahead of me."

-84-

Jeanne continued with her merry- go- round activities: home, office, stores, school, and home again.

She heard the phone ring as she opened the door to her apartment and ran to get it. Sara was on the other end.

"Are you all right? Where are you? I've been so worried. You missed Jeremy's birthday party." As usual Sara spoke without taking a breath.

"Oh shit. I'm so sorry -- it slipped my mind. I don't even know what today's date is..."

Sara became angry after she heard that her mother was all right. "I'm glad you're OK, but Mom, what's going on? Work's replacing us? I get to see you once in a while when I shop and need your discount, but Brianna and Jeremy don't know what happened to you. 'Where's Grandma,' Jeremy asked me today. 'Did she go away? She forgot my birthday? No present...' "

"Sorry, my sweet! I didn't realize how engrossed I've been and how much I've neglected all of you. I'll rectify it at once -- dinner tomorrow night -- my treat. And by the way, I have a surprise for you."

Sara's voice was cold and impersonal. "It'll have to wait. We have parent teacher night. Unfortunately your conscience will not be eased today -- maybe next week."

Jeanne heard the hurt in her daughter's voice. "Sara, I'm so sorry. Can I talk to Jeremy?"

"You don't even realize the time. He's fast asleep."

Jeanne had a sinking feeling in the pit of her stomach. *What's happened to me? I've become so involved I've forgotten how to live.* She slumped into a melancholy funk, and as the sadness set in she suddenly felt confined and difficult to breathe. *I need to get out of here.*

Once on the sidewalk, she took a deep breath of the warm air. Jeanne became aware of the summer night with the sky brightly illuminated by millions of stars; the moon still large enough added to the brightness. Sounds of music filtered the air and she found herself following the source. There was an outdoor concert of "50's music" in the gazebo of the neighborhood park. People gathered around the bandstand.

Wherever she turned she saw couples sway to the rhythm of the music, arms around each other -- bodies entwined -- sitting close together -- families singing. *It seems as if the whole world has someone; but not me.* Not allowing herself to cry, she willed herself to listen to the familiar tunes and thoughts soon turned to Ramon and how much they both enjoyed the 'Do-wop sounds.' His car radio was always tuned to this popular music. She remembered the times they relished it together and how much fun when she finally got him to 'twist.' A smile escaped.

*

Back in her own apartment Jeanne checked the day's receipts and entered them in the computer. She very often brought work home. Since it was her program she was fluent in the process and was done in a short time; very pleased with the success of the stores.

Homework was next on her list. She read through a few pages in her management book, retained none of the information, slammed it shut, and put it in her Gucci schoolbag. *Tomorrow is another night.* A feeling of fatigue overtook her. Suddenly she needed something to quell the lonely feeling that enveloped her. An old black and white movie and a dish of butter pecan will do it for me, she decided. She pressed the clicker to her favorite stations; it seemed as if love stories were the themes. Not even a good comedy to release me. Stop feeling sorry for yourself. She forced herself to concentrate on the dish in front of her. As the sweet cream melted in her mouth, she thought look what I've accomplished --a successful new career -- pursuing a baccalaureate degree-- a lovely apartment -- expensive clothes -- a great family.

"I'm an independent woman," she announced and forced a smile.

*

As the shower cascaded over her body, tears intermingled with the water. Memories of the times she shared the shower; the feel of his hands on her back as he soaped her body. She closed her eyes and could see how strong and taut his body was.

Jeanne hugged herself in the soft lilac bath sheet and inhaled to try to recapture his musky fragrance. He was all around her, but damn it -- not here at all.

Once in bed, she burrowed her head in the smooth pillow and flung her arm across the side of the crisp sheet. *How empty it is -- how cold! A big bed should be shared. I only sleep in a little corner, maybe a smaller one...*

Dreams invaded her slumber. In her dream, Jeanne was outside of a crowd of people. Voices emanated.

"Become an independent woman," her mother whined. "Do it for me..."

Then Sam stepped up and cried, "Come home with me, forty years together..."

"Grandma, where are you? I miss you..."

"Mom..."

She ran around in circles and found herself searching the crowd. A dark haired man, his back to her, spoke in a strong voice, "Join me. I love you. I need you, querida."

She tried to go to him but couldn't catch him. Things kept getting in the way. He disappeared in the throngs...

Sunlight flooded the room and Jeanne woke with a start. ... She gave an involuntary shudder; and realized she had turned into a lonely, self-assured person; the hollowness of material success. What price glory?

"Independent woman, Hell!" She picked up the phone..."Ramon?"

Made in the USA
Middletown, DE
27 February 2015